TY'S TEMPTATION

BAD IN BOOTS SERIES

P.T. MICHELLE
PATRICE MICHELLE

LIMITLESS INK PRESS, LLC

TY'S TEMPTATION (BOOK 2)

BY P.T. MICHELLE & PATRICE MICHELLE

BAD IN BOOTS Series
Reading Order

Harm's Hunger
Ty's Temptation
Colt's Choice
Josh's Justice

Note: Harm's Hunger is the only novella. All the other books are novel length. Every book in the series can be read as a stand alone story

Good things come to those who wait...

COPYRIGHT

To stay informed when the next **P.T. Michelle** book will be released, join P.T.'s free newsletter http://bit.ly/11tqAQN

SUMMARY

With a genius IQ, Evan Masters has always been one step ahead of most people, except when it comes to matters of the heart. When she stumbles across a seductive, tightly controlled man visiting town for a short time, she realizes he's the perfect person to show her the ropes with no strings attached.

Ty Hudson agrees to teach Evan all he knows about sex, but he insists on doing it his way, slow and easy. As their sensual dance turns into a smoldering burn, Ty quickly discovers that innocent "Eve" is more temptation than he can resist.

The books in the BAD IN BOOTS series can be read as stand alone stories. Reading order of the BAD IN BOOTS series, which is best suited for mature readers:

COLT'S CHOICE (Book 3 - Novel)
JOSH'S JUSTICE (Book 4 - Novel)

1

"Is that your car?"

Ty finished paying for his soda and turned to the blond teen who'd tapped him on the shoulder. "What?"

The kid tilted his head toward the gas station parking lot. "Is that your red convertible?"

Ty unscrewed the cap and nodded, giving him an indulgent smile. He took a long swig and enjoyed the brief relief the cool beverage provided from the fall Texas heat. Letting out a sigh of satisfaction, he twisted the lid back on. "It's a rental, but it's my car while I'm visiting."

The sound of squealing tires screeched through the open door, and the boy smirked. "Looks like it's someone else's car now."

Ty jerked his gaze to the parking lot in time to see the taillights of his rented sports car shoot into traffic. His heart raced and anger quickly slammed to the surface. "Why didn't you say something sooner?"

The boy shrugged as he put his candy bar on the counter.

"Hey, I just saw him get into the convertible. I didn't know if the guy was with you or not."

Ty mentally counted to ten while he jangled his keys in front of the kid. "Seeing him hotwire my car didn't clue you in?"

The teenager handed his money to the young female cashier, who was listening to their conversation with avid interest. Peeling away the wrapper, he took a bite out of his candy bar. The strong smell of peanuts and chocolate drifted Ty's way as the boy spoke, "Maybe you shouldn't have left your top down."

Ty DROVE along the tree-lined dirt road that led to his great-aunt Sally's Double D ranch. Gravel crunched under his tires as he rolled to a halt in the driveway in front of the small one-story house. He climbed out of the cramped, two-seater sports car and grimaced, pressing his palm against his stiff spine. *That'll teach me to ask for the first available convertible.* Pulling his cell from his pocket, he leaned on the car's hood and dialed Jena's number.

"It's about time, Ty!"

"Heya, Sis. I'm at the Double D. Thanks for sending the key."

"Where have you been? I tried your cell, but you must've left it turned off. I expected you to come by Steele Way and have lunch with us hours ago. We've held off the wedding for a couple of months now while you finished your project...and you take your sweet time getting here? I want you to see

Harm's ranch and spend some time getting to know my fiancé."

"That 'project' was a eight-million-dollar, state-of-the-art building, Jena. It raised Hudson & Shannon's reputation in the architectural community several notches." Ty rubbed the back of his neck, feeling the weight of the three-hour police interview and annoying paperwork with the car rental agency starting to take its toll. "I'll see you tomorrow, bright and early. Let's just say I've had a hell of a day. I want to hit the hay early tonight."

"Is everything all right?"

He ran a hand through his hair and down the five o'clock shadow on his jaw, chuckling. "Yeah. Apparently the Hudsons don't have the best of luck with rental cars."

"Oh no! Did your car die on you, too?"

"Worse. It was stolen."

"You're kidding me!"

Ty gave a tired sigh. "I wish I were."

"I'm so sorry. Do you need us to come get you?"

"No, I've got another car, but I'll see you tomorrow as promised."

"Okay. Get some rest."

Ty put his phone away and opened the car door to pull out his suitcase. The empty backseat was a jarring reminder his suitcase was still in the stolen car, including his custom made suit. "I hope he's too short for my clothes," he grumbled as he headed for the front door.

As soon as he walked inside, Ty noticed two things—Jena kept her promise to have the place ready for him, and he couldn't get enough of the smell permeating the room. Cinnamon and apples.

Glancing to the left of the entryway to the kitchen, he grinned when he saw a pie sitting on the stove. His sister knew how much he loved apple pie. The kitchen flowed right into the living room, where he and Jena had spent many hours playing card games with their great aunt and toasting marshmallows in the stone fireplace. A big picture window took up the wall straight ahead of him. The door farthest away opened to the only bedroom. The door next to it led to a two-way bathroom that served as the bedroom and guest bathroom.

When his attention circled back to the small, efficient kitchen, with its wooden table and four mission-style chairs, he smiled in memory of his and Jena's past summer visits with their Aunt Sally. He didn't even mind that he spent his nights sleeping on a foldout cot so Jena could have the sofa bed.

You'd better wash those hands and freshen up before you dare to sit at my table. His aunt's stern, but loving voice entered his head as if it were yesterday and not twenty years since he'd last seen her.

"I miss your spunky self, Aunt Sal," he murmured, regretting he didn't get a chance to see her before she passed away.

Ty started toward the bathroom, and as he walked past the end table next to the couch, he noticed the paring knife and plate his sister had forgotten to take back to the kitchen. Shaking his head, he chuckled. Some things never changed. Growing up, Jena had always forgotten to put her dishes away.

As soon as he put his hand on the bathroom's doorknob, the door jerked open. A tall woman, wearing nothing but a fluffy white towel, walked out of the bathroom.

"Aaaaahh!" She took a step back, her mouth a tiny "O" of shock.

Ty raised his hands. "Hey, I—"

Before he had a chance to finish, she ripped off the towel, then threw the cloth over his head, blocking his view.

Heart racing from the unexpected scenario, Ty reached to grab the towel from his face. A jolting blow to the back of his knees caused his legs to buckle. Another hit behind his ankles sent his feet flying. As he landed flat on his back, air whooshed out of his lungs. *What the hell?* Still reeling, he heard a loud crash on the floor. Adrenaline thrummed through him as he started to remove the towel, but instead of finding freedom, his wrists, then his ankles were quickly bound with something thin yet strong.

When the towel flew off his face, Ty rolled over ceramic shards on the wood floor as he struggled against what appeared to be an electrical cord binding.

The woman leaned over him. One hand clutched the towel to her breasts and the other held a paring knife pointed at his throat. "Move another inch and you'll find out the hard way I'm not afraid to stick you like the trussed-up pig you are." Straightening, she backed away, her movements slow and cautious.

Water dripped from her hair onto the delicate slope of her shoulders, disappearing in the valley between her breasts. Now that she'd stopped moving, he realized her hair was a light color. Strawberry-blonde maybe?

Obviously he'd scared the shit out of her. Despite the misunderstanding, Ty was impressed by her quick reflexes and instinctive defensive responses.

He met her angry gaze and stared. She had the most unusual, mesmerizing eyes; robin's-egg blue, flecked with shades of gold and brown. "I believe you're trespassing," he said in a calm voice.

"*I'm* trespassing." She frowned. "You're the one who's trespassing. I was invited."

Ty raised an eyebrow. "So was I."

Her delicate golden brows drew together. "By whom?"

"By my sister. She owns this place."

"Jena's your sister?"

Ty smiled at the squeak in her voice. The pink tinge that colored her cheeks was so sincere.

He nodded. "I'm Ty Hudson."

"Oh, my God! I'm so sorry." Setting the knife on the plate on the end table, she turned her back to wrap the towel around herself.

Ty grinned at the brief glimpse he got of her perfect ass.

Turning back, she kneeled next to him. As she untied the electrical cord from around his ankles, she said, "Harm invited me to stay here."

Anger sliced through him. "Harm?" It had only been two months since Harm asked Jena to marry him. The man better not have a woman on the side or he would have to kill the bastard!

His expression must've reflected his thoughts, because she quickly explained, "Harm had problems with one of Sally's horses. With the wedding days away and his attention otherwise occupied, I volunteered to stay here to keep an eye on the mare and make sure she's healing fine."

As she leaned over him to undo the knot at his wrists, water dripped onto his dress shirt. Not that he cared. He was too busy enjoying the scent teasing his nostrils—cinnamon and vanilla. Damn, she smelled good. And here he thought cinnamon and apples smelled like heaven. *Her* scent had just blown that theory to smithereens. He

6

inhaled once, twice, three times, drinking in her intoxicating aroma.

She looked at him, concern in her gaze. "Are you okay? Did I tie you too tight?"

When the last of the cord slid off him, she started to pull away. Ty grabbed her wrist. Grinning, he lowered his voice. "You're welcome to tie me up anytime you want."

Color bloomed on her cheeks once more, making him realize he hadn't seen such a genuine reaction in a woman in a very long time. His suspicions kicked in. Full force. She had to be around twenty-five or so. No way she was *that* innocent.

Without responding, she used his hold on her wrist to help pull him to his feet.

Once they stood facing one another, Ty's grip loosened, yet he still didn't want to release her. Despite the warning bells clanging in his head, he felt a sudden urge to learn everything about her. "You never told me your name."

EVAN'S HEART raced and electricity hummed when he slid his fingers slowly down her wrist, then traced his thumb along her palm.

Concentrating on answering, instead of the intense physical awareness he ignited, helped her regain focus. "I'm Evan Masters."

"Nice to meet you, Miss. Masters." Ty lifted her left hand and turned it over, planting a kiss on her open palm.

Whether he meant it or not, his kiss had felt so intimate, her stomach flip-flopped. Evan's gaze landed on his short, silky dark hair, skimmed the starched blue cotton shirt that stretched across broad shoulders, then moved to his gray dress slacks and Italian leather shoes. The man's impeccable, expensive clothes were a stark contrast to the worn jeans and casual tank top that awaited her on the bed in the bedroom.

"Um, I hope we can start over. That wasn't my best first impression."

His vivid green gaze held a dark, intense look before his eyebrows rose in amusement. "At least I'm now versed in how well you can defend yourself."

She gave a sheepish smile. "My dad made sure I knew how to take care of myself."

Ty glanced at the gutted table lamp. Bits of blue ceramic scattered across the floor and the ripped-out electrical cord now lay in an innocent tangle on the floor. "I might've gotten knocked off my feet and all tied up, but I think the lamp got the worse of it."

Evan glanced at the lamp pieces and grimaced. "Looks like I'll be buying Jena a new lamp."

When Ty chuckled, she felt inordinately pleased that she had made him smile. For the first time in her life, a man grabbed her rapt attention. Correction...this particular man made her tingle and ache everywhere. And this reaction was triggered by nothing more than a complimentary comment and a blatant sexy gaze. *My God, what would he be like when he really turned on the charm?*

As Ty stared at her...and a knowing smile tilted his lips, Evan ground her teeth. Why'd she have to be such an easy read?

Clearing her throat, she tried to sound casual as she backed away, "It was nice to meet you, Ty. I'll clean the lamp up after I get dressed."

TY WATCHED Evan bolt from the room and shut the bedroom door behind her. *Interesting development.* Once he was no longer distracted by her presence, the delicious smell of the apple pie drew his attention. He picked up the knife and plate from the end table and carried them into the kitchen. Setting the dirty plate and utensil on the counter, he crouched next to the sink and opened the two doors underneath it. Yep, the hand broom and dustpan were still in the same spot they were twenty years ago. During his summer stays, his aunt made sure he knew how to use them, too. Grabbing them, Ty walked over to the lamp's mess on the floor.

After he'd swept up the broken pieces, then dumped the rest of the lamp and electrical cord into the tall trashcan inside the small pantry, Ty retrieved a clean plate from the cabinet. When he took that first bite, he closed his eyes at the delicious taste. The flavors of cinnamon and apples blended perfectly. *Jena has really learned to cook over the years,* he thought, remembering all the dinners his sister had botched when they were teens.

"Making yourself at home, I see," Evan's voice sounded from behind him.

Ty turned in his chair at the table, fork poised next to his mouth. "I take it Jena didn't make this pie for me?"

She shook her head, lips twisted in amusement. "But I'm glad to see someone enjoying it. I usually only cook when I'm trying to work something out in my head. I find it therapeutic." She gestured toward him. "Go ahead. You deserve it after cleaning up the mess I made. Guess I owe your sister a lamp."

Now that her hair was dry, Ty realized the color was as he suspected—a gorgeous strawberry blonde. He smiled his appreciation of her cooking and took another bite. "You make a fantastic apple pie."

Evan grinned. "Thanks. I'm glad you like it."

As she set a backpack down on the floor next to her chair, his gaze locked on the silver Labrador tag that jostled back and forth against the blue fabric. "Are you an animal lover?"

Evan followed his line of sight to her backpack zipper pull. "I guess you could say that. I'm kind of...an assistant vet."

"If Harm's horse needs constant attention, why isn't the vet tending to it?"

Evan retrieved another plate and fork. "He's out of town on vacation for a couple of weeks, so I'm filling in for him," she replied, then cut herself a slice of pie and sat down across from him.

"If he trusts you enough to take his place while he's not here, why don't you go to school and get your degree. Then you can either open your own practice or partner with him. At least that way you'd get all the benefits."

"And all the full-time responsibility!" Evan replied with a chuckle, knowing full well just how much.

"There's that," he agreed.

There was something about this man. She couldn't put her finger on it, but she didn't want him thinking she was some kind of brainiac. If he learned she was the town's vet, he'd question how young she looked. Then he'd inevitably find out she had graduated from high school at sixteen, and accelerated through college and vet school, earning both her MBA and a DVM, before graduating at the young age of twenty-four. Would he react the way most men did? If so, she'd have a strike against her. In her limited and disappointing experience with men, the male population shied away from women with extremely high IQs.

She was about to take her first bite of pie when her cell phone rang. "Duty calls." Evan gave Ty a half-smile as she jumped up to retrieve her cell phone from her backpack.

"Hello...Hey, Charlie. When did her water break? The front hooves aren't coming out first? No, don't try to turn the foal yourself. I'll be there in a few minutes. Just keep the momma calm."

When she snapped the phone closed, Ty glanced at his watch. "You should consider my suggestion. It seems you're on call 24/7 anyway."

She gave a wry grin. "I'll take it under advisement." Picking up her backpack, she met his gaze. "I'll collect my things and leave the place to you."

"If Harm invited you, I don't want to kick you out."

"No worries. I'll just drive over each morning and evening." Pulling the house key off her keychain, she set it on the table.

"Evan—"

Her cell phone rang again. "Hold that thought." She raised her finger and answered the phone.

"Hello? Yes, I can squeeze you in. Bring Ranger by the office tomorrow morning. I'll be in at nine."

When she hung up, Ty raised an eyebrow. "I think that vet needs more help."

She grinned and turned to walk toward the bedroom to collect her things, calling over her shoulder, "Yeah, he stays pretty busy."

2

Three hours later, Evan rolled down her window as she approached her house. Even though Charlie had let her use the shower in his guest bathroom to get cleaned up, and she now had on the spare set of clothes she carried around in her car, the scent of childbirth, sweat, manure and hay still filled her nose. She inhaled, welcoming the fall night air. The smell brought a nostalgic memory of skinny-dipping in Sweet Trails Lake and feeling the chill as the fall season cooled down the water a few degrees.

When she saw a red pickup truck sitting in her driveway and Chad's blond head through the back window, her stomach tensed and she let out a deep sigh. Pushing on the gas, she drove right past her house. She'd gone out with Chad a couple times a few months ago. She'd been attracted to the fact the guy showed no fear of her father. Evan quickly learned Chad's fearlessness had nothing to do with bravery, but everything to do with the fact Chad's father was mayor.

She thought she'd seen confidence in Chad. The truth

was, he not only thumbed his nose at authority, but he walked around with a cocky confidence that wore thin very quickly. He was easy on the eyes, but it took more than looks for Evan. She'd turned Chad down when he'd asked her out for a third date. For a man who'd always gotten his way with ladies, he'd seemed to take it as a personal affront that she'd refused to sleep with him. Apparently he'd thought their third date would be his lucky night.

Ever since then, Chad had periodically shown up and asked her to go out with him. A couple of weeks ago, on the same day she received an invitation to Harm and Jena's wedding, Chad called and asked her to be his date at their wedding. So far he didn't seem to want to take "no" for an answer. She didn't feel threatened in any way—just annoyed—but she had a feeling the guy would hound her about it until she gave in. He seemed damned determined to add her to his list of conquests. She suspected the fact she was a virgin only made her more of a prize in Chad's eyes.

Turning her SUV around in the cul-de-sac at the end of the street, she hoped Ty meant what he said about not wanting to kick her out. Sharing a house with Jena's sexy brother sounded like a great way to remain out-of-sight for a few more days. She was too busy at her office for Chad to bother her there.

Once she'd parked her car by the stables, Evan walked into the building to check on Harm's horse. She unwrapped Flash's hurt leg and massaged the swollen area. At least she didn't feel any heat, which would indicate infection. The swelling was almost gone. In another day, she'd take Flash back to Steele Way for some limited exercise. She knew Flash missed frolicking with the other horses. After tomorrow's jaunt, Evan would know if Flash was ready to go back to the ranch full-time. She replaced the binding back, gave Flash a pat, then retrieved her backpack from her car.

As she quietly made her way to the house, Evan glanced at her watch. It was nine-thirty and the house was dark. Ty must've turned in early. Now she wished she'd held onto the Double D house key, so she could quietly let herself in without waking Ty.

There was another way.

The front door didn't have a deadbolt, just the main door lock. Setting her backpack on the porch, she unzipped it and pulled a credit card from her wallet. She'd seen this technique on TV once and wasn't sure if it'd work or not, but it was worth a try.

Biting her lip, she carefully slid the stiff card between the door and the weather-stripping right where the latch would be. With careful movements, she grasped the doorknob with one hand and maneuvered the credit card with the other until she felt the latch give way. Evan exhaled a sigh of relief that she'd successfully unlocked the door.

The cool air-conditioning caused chill bumps to form on her arms. Sheesh, the man must run very hot. *Now there's an intriguing idea*, she thought with a twist of her lips. Her fun musings were suddenly cut off when someone grabbed her by the neck. Before she could utter a word, she was slammed against the open front door, a hard body pressing against her.

Dropping her bag, Evan brought her knee up, expecting to nail her attacker in the groin. Instead she met a muscular thigh as the man backed up a little to block her move.

"Evan? Are you trying to get yourself killed?" Ty hissed in

the dark. He released her neck and grasped her bare arms in a tight grip.

As her heart slammed against her ribcage, Evan's eyes quickly adjusted to the moonlight filtering through the front door. Involuntarily sliding her gaze down Ty's broad chest to his trim, well-defined abs, she quickly yanked her attention back to his intense gaze, thankful he at least had his dress pants on.

"I was trying not to wake you. I didn't expect to be attacked," she shot back, tension edging her voice. It was hard to shake off being caught so completely off-guard.

Ty's grip on her arms loosened and he took a step closer. "I thought you said you were going home." As he spoke, his fingers trailed down her arms and a half-smile tilted the corners of his lips.

When he glanced at her tank top's spaghetti straps as if he wanted to plant a kiss on her shoulder, Ty's scent caught her attention. He smelled so good, like sandalwood and musky male. She took a deep breath just to pull more of his smell in. But it wasn't just the way he smelled, the husky timbre in his voice made her heart rate rev, not to mention his towering height. He stood a good four inches taller than her five-foot-ten height. *Perfect*, she thought as her stomach fluttered at his nearness.

"Um, something came up and I decided if you didn't mind sharing a house with me for a couple of days, I'd stay." What would he say if she told him he set her senses on fire? There was just something about his quiet, intense approach that caused her to tingle all over.

A frown creased his brow and his expression turned serious. "I like my privacy."

Guess she wasn't going to find out. Her stomach pitched and disappointment rushed like lead filling her stomach. She started to pick up the bag she'd dropped. "Okay, I'll leave—"

The pressure of Ty's fingers on her chin caused her to pause and meet his gaze.

"But I'd be willing to make an exception."

The deep register of his voice, followed by his fingers skimming down her neck, sent a shiver of heated response down her spine.

"Is that an invitation?" She knew she sounded caught up, but she didn't care.

"Tell me why you're hiding out here. Maybe I can help."

His intimate touch drew her in. Evan's breath caught at the heat emanating off his skin. This sexy man was giving her exactly what she wanted; the beginnings of an attraction between a man and a woman. No preconceived notions. No worry that she could run circles around him on an IQ level. Nothing but pure and honest desire zinged between them.

The way he made her feel—breathless and totally intrigued—she realized he was the perfect man to help her. Though she was pretty sure he wasn't offering the kind of "help" she currently needed, she hoped it wouldn't be too hard to convince him. He was only temporarily in Texas, so it's not like he would think she'd expect anything more from him.

Before she could speak, he put his hand on the door behind her and leaned a bit closer. "Tell me what changed your mind."

His encouraging voice instantly put her at ease. She couldn't believe how comfortable she felt with a man she'd just met, but she did. Evan placed her hands tentatively on his bare chest. She couldn't resist, he was so beautiful. When her skin touched his, his warmth shot straight to her toes.

"I just prefer to avoid an old boyfriend who's determined to have me as his date at your sister's wedding. Once the wedding's over, I'm pretty sure he'll stop hounding me."

Ty narrowed his gaze suspiciously for a brief moment, then he pulled her away from the door. "Looks like we'll be sharing quarters for a few days." Picking up the backpack she'd dropped when he'd grabbed her, he followed her inside and kicked the door closed with his foot.

Facing Ty in the dark, Evan was suddenly unsure what to say next. Silence stretched for a long, heated moment. The attraction arcing between them wove through the air, making the tiny hairs on her arms stand on end.

"I'll take the couch," she offered, her voice sounding unusually high.

"I think it'll be a tight fit."

"Huh?"

"That's where I'm sleeping. You can have the bed."

"I don't want to kick you out of your bed."

"You could always join me." His gaze locked with hers, blatant and honest.

Her heart galloped. Was he teasing her? It was hard to tell with his serious expression. "Um, I'll take the bed."

The corners of his lips tilted in amusement at her quick response. Handing her the bag, he said in a husky tone, "Sleep well."

Evan's fingers accidentally brushed his when she took the backpack. Her heart leapt and her breath hitched. She quickly glanced at him, hoping he hadn't heard.

Ty's penetrating gaze slid down her face, lingered at her breasts, then returned to her lips. "See you in the morning."

Even in the dim light, the heated look in his eyes told her he wanted to follow her to the bedroom. Heaven help her, she wanted him to. How could she be so attracted to a complete stranger?

She inhaled slowly to calm the rapid beating of her heart. "Thank you for your generosity. Good night."

ONCE EVAN CLOSED the bedroom door, Ty stretched out on the couch and folded his arms behind his head, contemplating her. Generosity? He chuckled at her comment. He was a selfish bastard through and through.

He could still smell her sweet vanilla and cinnamon scent, feel her warm body pressed to his, her generous breasts crushed against his chest while her heart beat at a rapid pace. He didn't think it'd take much to seduce Evan, but for some reason he didn't want to push her too fast. Maybe he liked anticipating just how she'd feel when he slid inside her. She was the perfect height, allowing for all kinds of sexual positions. His groin began to throb at the thought.

Evan looked nothing like the sophisticated women he normally slept with, yet there was something about her natural look...gorgeous shoulder-length wavy strawberry-blonde hair, wide-set sexy blue-brown eyes combined with the sprinkle of freckles across her nose made him hard as a rock as soon as he laid eyes on her. Not to mention she had a body he definitely wanted to explore from head to toe.

The blush he'd seen on her cheeks when he saw her naked made him think she hadn't had many sexual partners. Yet her self-confidence told him she'd probably be open to just about anything he dished out. A slow smile curved his lips as he instantly grew rock hard thinking about Evan.

When the ache in his balls turned almost painful, Ty closed his eyes and focused on taking deep, even breaths until his erection diminished. He welcomed the biting challenge to his body just as he looked forward to exploring anything and everything Evan would allow while he pushed her to the limits of her sexual bounds. The woman had no idea just what kind of man she was sharing a house with. He learned a long time ago to leave his emotions and his conscience at the door. "No inhibitions, no limits" was a motto he'd lived by.

He frowned when he thought of how quickly she'd tied him and shoved that knife in his face. Her confidence and sassy attitude didn't mesh with the story she told him about her old boyfriend. He intuitively knew she wasn't the kind of woman to hide from her problems. He'd find out the truth soon enough.

3

E van awoke to the sun just peeking over the horizon. The house was still. Which meant she'd have to be extra quiet making her morning cup of coffee so she wouldn't wake Ty. First she planned to check on and feed Flash, then maybe she'd take her for a slow walk today.

Evan slid into a pair of blue jeans and a baby blue tank top then pulled her wavy hair back into a quick ponytail. As she brushed her teeth, she critiqued her face in the mirror. She had big, wide-set eyes, her best feature as far as she was concerned. The unusual color combination tended to draw people's attention. Her nose was passable, not too big or too small, but she had a nice mouth. "Full lips," Chad had called them. The few times he'd kissed her, he'd tried to suck them. Maybe if she'd been attracted to him that would've been sexy. Instead it was a turn-off.

She removed her toothbrush from her mouth and took in her overall look. From her wavy hair to the tips of her toes, she was a farm-bred cowgirl. What would a city-fied guy like Ty, with his expensive, starched cotton shirts, silk-blend pants and Italian leather shoes, see in her?

She spit the toothpaste in the sink, then stuck her tongue out at herself in the mirror. Nothing.

Disappointed, she turned to walk out of the bathroom and caught a glimpse of her rear in the mirror. She definitely had a nice ass in jeans. A broad smile replaced her frown. *Work with what you've got, girl*, she told herself as she flipped the light switch off.

When she walked into an empty living room, Evan glanced around in surprise. *Where could Ty be?* Casting her gaze past the linen curtains over the sink as she pulled down a bag of coffee from the cabinet, she spotted his car. He had to be here somewhere.

Movement to the right of the driveway drew her attention. Ty stood thirty feet away, facing the rising sun. His chest and feet were bare, but he still wore the pants he had on yesterday. He moved using precise hand and foot actions, as if he were doing some kind of solo martial arts practice. His back muscles rippled with each calculated stretch and turn.

Evan marveled as she watched his fluid movements. They were so mesmerizing, she had to tear her gaze away to get moving on making the coffee.

When the smell of fresh-brewed coffee began to waft through the air, Evan inhaled, enjoying the rich scent. As much as she loved coffee, she often thought it smelled better brewing than it actually tasted. At least until she added cream and sugar, she mentally amended with a smile as she opened the cabinet once more to pull down a coffee cup.

Just as her hand gripped the ceramic cup, warm fingers

surrounded hers at the same time. How'd he get inside so fast and without her hearing him enter?

"This has to be the sexiest backside I've seen in a very long time," he whispered in her ear while he lowered their hands, cup and all, to the counter. "Morning, Evan."

The man sure knew how to make an entrance. A shiver coursed through her as she stared at his hand covering hers. Though only his hand touched her, he was close enough that she literally felt his heat from her shoulders to the base of her spine. His musky scent made her electrify all over.

When he pulled away, she turned to face him and raised an eyebrow at the sheen of sweat that coated his chest and dampened the fringes of his close-cropped hair.

"You were working out?"

He flashed a smile, then nodded toward the coffeepot. "You make enough for two?"

Evan retrieved another coffee cup and filled it to the brim. Intuitively she knew this man took his coffee black. As she handed him the cup and watched him take his first sip, she took a moment to appreciate his well-defined abs in the early morning light. Her stomach fluttered when she wondered...*what would it feel like to have those abs pressed against me in more than just a teasing manner?* The fact he worked out in his dress pants, not caring a whit that he sweated all over the expensive material surprised her. Was there a bit of the country boy in Ty? Come to think of it...why *hadn't* he changed to workout?

She gestured with her empty cup toward him. "You exercise in your dress clothes often?"

Ty glanced at his attire with a grimace. "Only when my rental car is stolen with my suitcase in it."

Evan winced. "Sorry! I didn't know."

Ty took a sip of his coffee and leaned against the counter. "I just hope they find the car and my suitcase soon or I'll be doing some shopping."

When he finished speaking, Ty continued to stare at her over his coffee cup. Those green eyes seemed to read so much, to peer right though her, scanning her innermost thoughts. Turning back to the coffeepot, she murmured, "Why don't you sit down and I'll make us some breakfast."

"Got something on your mind?"

"What?" She glanced back to see the right side of his mouth lifted in amusement.

He gestured toward the stove. "You. Cooking. Stuff on your mind?"

A flush stole over her cheeks. She'd forgotten that she'd told him she cooked when she was mulling over something. "I'm just hungry. I figured feeding you is the least I can do for you allowing me to stay here."

The look in Ty's eyes shifted and the green color turned darker. "I look forward to tasting what you offer up," he said in a husky tone before he turned and sat down at the table.

"Just sit tight. I'll have breakfast done in no time," she said in a bright voice. Her heart racing, Evan turned back to the stove and withdrew the skillet from the drawer below. The man was just too sexy for words. God, he was way out of her league. She was insane to think she'd have anything to offer him. Sure, she knew her own body, but she was inexperienced when it came to knowing what a man wanted...well, other than to get off as fast as he possibly could. Was that written in a how-to-be-a-man manual somewhere?

She opened the fridge and retrieved the bacon, then laid a

few pieces of meat in the hot skillet, her mind whirling. But the good part was...if she made a fool of herself, Ty wouldn't be around to remind her of it. No matter how tense she felt over bringing the subject up with Ty, she refused to talk herself out of this idea. While she turned the bacon with a fork, she felt even more certain Ty was perfect—in every since of the word. The man obviously wanted to pursue something with her. She'd be a fool not to take him up on it.

Once she'd set the cooked bacon on a napkin-lined plate, Evan pulled out the carton of eggs from the fridge and cracked a few eggs in the pan. While she scrambled the eggs with a spatula, her confidence built. She knew she was making the right decision.

After she'd placed the full plate in front of him, Ty picked up his fork and dug into the food with gusto, commenting, "I don't usually eat such a large breakfast."

Evan sat down across from him with her own plate and utensils. She picked up her fork. "Me either. I'm usually too busy."

"With your job?" Ty asked as he popped a forkful of eggs into his mouth.

She took a bite of her bacon and nodded.

Ty tilted his head to the side, contemplating her. "Why don't you go back to school and get your vet license? Then you can open up your own business."

That was the second time he mentioned she should strive to own the veterinary business. He seemed really bothered by the fact she deserved more out of her job, that she wasn't working to her full potential. Then again, from his comments to her about her own career and the expensive clothes he wore, Ty appeared to be the type of man who worked hard to get to the top of the ladder. She'd lay money on the fact he was a high level executive.

"So what do you do?" she asked him.

Ty picked up a piece of bacon and bit into it. "I'm part owner of a company in Maryland."

"Ah, I was right."

His brow creased. "About what?"

She smiled. "That you're a driven, career-minded person."

"And that's a bad thing?"

"Not at all. I was just making a comment."

"You're right. I'm a Classic A type, driven to succeed." His voice dropped to a seductive purr. "In every aspect in my life."

She couldn't miss the sexual connotation of his tone. Now was as good a time as any, Evan thought. "About the offer you made to help me yesterday..."

Ty's fork paused on the way to his mouth, his expression intrigued.

She plowed forward before she lost her courage. "I could use your help in one area. You know the boyfriend I told you about last night?"

Ty nodded.

"I think you could help get him off my back once and for all."

"How can I help you?" he asked before he took another bite of eggs.

"You can sleep with me."

Ty's gaze jerked to hers and he choked on his food.

Alarmed, Evan jumped up and came around the table to touch his shoulder. "Are you okay?"

Still coughing, he nodded and met her gaze. "You want me to have sex with you to get rid of your boyfriend?"

Her cheeks flamed and she gave an uncomfortable laugh. "I guess that sounded kind of weird, huh?"

He grabbed her around the waist and pulled her into his lap. "Baby, I'll be more than happy to accommodate you, but I have to know why my having sex with you would make your old boyfriend leave you alone."

Relief flooded through her that he'd agreed. Placing her hands on his broad shoulders, Evan laughed. "Getting rid of this blasted virginity once and for all should make Chad go away. I think he sees it as some kind of trophy to notch into his bedpost of conquests. So once it's gone, he'll just see me as any other woman and move on."

As soon as she said the word "virginity", Ty's shoulders tensed under her hands.

Setting her back on the floor, he adopted a closed expression. "I'm sorry, but virgins are where I draw the line."

His rejection hit her like a slap in the face. She was the one who had a reason to be offended, so why the hell was a muscle jumping in his jaw. He wasn't looking at her any longer either. She knew Ty was attracted to her and he still wanted her, even if he had some hang-up against virgins. Damn him! No way was she going to let him put a brick wall between them. If he wanted to see her "meet her full potential", the man was about to find out just how determined she could be when she set her mind to something.

She crossed her arms. "What's wrong, Ty? You have something against virgins?"

He met her gaze, anger flashing in the deep green depths. "Virgins expect more and I'm not into commitment."

"No worries there. I only asked you *because* you're here for the short-term."

Something flared in Ty's gaze. Interest? Was he caving? She had a feeling this man couldn't resist a challenge.

Evan put her hands on her hips. "Tell you what. How about a little wager? I challenge you to a wrestling match. If you pin me for ten seconds, I'll drop my request. But if I win, you'll follow through."

Ty's eyes narrowed, suspicion reflected in his gaze.

"Surely you don't think you'll lose? To a *girl!*"

A broad grin spread across Ty's face as he stood to his full height. Staring down at her, he said in a low tone, "I'm going to enjoy pinning you."

So cocky! She tilted her chin. "How quickly you forget who had whom trussed up like a pig yesterday."

Ty raised a dark eyebrow, then swept his arm toward the living room where they'd have a little space. "You're welcome to try your best, Miss."

Evan preceded him into the living room and quickly became irritated at the formal tone he'd adopted, as if he were already putting distance between them. Her narrowed gaze tracked Ty as he moved the sofa and chair back to give them room.

Ty walked around her in a slow circle as if he were stalking his prey. She didn't give him the satisfaction of seeing her gaze trace his steps. She knew he was there, waiting.

"Are you ready?" Ty's deep voice came from directly behind her.

She didn't respond. Instead, she swiftly dropped to a squat and swept her leg behind her, hooking his ankles.

Ty stumbled, but kept his footing. "Nice try."

He grinned at her once she'd straightened and faced him.

"Are you going to tell me why you're still a virgin at...what are you? Twenty-five?"

They each circled, looking for a weak spot.

"I'm twenty-six and why I'm still a virgin is none of your damn business." Evan lunged at him, trying to take him off balance.

He used her momentum against her and before she knew what had happened she was flat on her back with Ty's body covering hers.

Evan tried to use her legs to shove him off, but Ty wrapped his legs around hers, locking them in place. His naked chest pressed against her thin T-shirt, making her very aware of his heat and sexy smell.

The amused look fled his face, replaced by a serious one when he met her annoyed gaze. "You can tell me now."

"It's not important. Let me up."

Ty stared at her for a long moment as if he debated whether to push the issue. "Not until you say Uncle."

Annoyed he'd so thoroughly bested her, Evan began to squirm in earnest to be released. Did he *have* to rub it in?

He just held her tighter. "Go ahead, Evan...say Uncle."

"No," she gritted out, exerting herself once more.

TY WAS INTRIGUED by the stubborn streak that ran through Evan. He wanted to learn more about her. What drove her? Why *hadn't* she gone on with her education to get her vet's license? She didn't appear the type who was afraid of hard work. If the way she refused to back down in their wrestle match was any indication, she had a strong will. One thing he knew for sure, she felt damn good underneath him. Why the hell did she have to be a blasted virgin?

"You're so stubborn. Concede. Say Uncle."

Her cheeks flushed with her exertions, she shook her head and started to say, "Nev—" when something in her eyes changed and her voice pitched higher. "Daddy!"

Ty chuckled. "I might be ten years older than you, but 'Uncle' will do."

Someone cleared his throat behind him, and Ty glanced over his shoulder to see a tall, barrel-chested man with salt and pepper hair. He stood with his arms crossed, a deep scowl creasing his face.

When the morning sunlight reflected off the sheriff's badge on the man's chest, Ty shook his head. If the situation didn't look so bad, it'd be funny.

"There better be a damn good reason you have my daughter held to the floor, son!"

Ty quickly let go of Evan and stood, pulling her to her feet. "Good morning, Sheriff," he said, extending his hand. "Was just showing Evan some aikido moves."

The older man ignored his hand and pinned his gaze on Evan. "What are you doing here, Evelyn?"

She walked to her father's side and gave him a quick hug. "I could ask you the same thing."

"I'm here on business." Her dad frowned. When he flicked his gaze to Ty, his frown deepened.

"Me too," she shot back with a grin.

Ty almost choked when the man's gaze swept his bare chest, then narrowed to angry slits.

Evan glanced from Ty to her dad. "Ty, this is my father, Jake Masters. Dad, this is Ty Hudson, Jena's brother."

"I know who he is," her dad said in a curt tone, looking at Ty. "I'm here to tell you we've found your stolen rental car. I'll take you to town so you can get all the paperwork signed, and then we'll release your belongings to you."

Glancing at his daughter, he continued in a suspicious voice, "Why are you here so early?"

"Because I'm st—"

"She's here to look after Harm's horse," Ty interrupted. The last thing he needed was the man arresting him for "living in sin" with his daughter.

The sheriff cut his gaze to Evan. "You are?"

She nodded. "I promised Harm I'd look out for Flash until she's able to go back with the other horses."

Her father snorted, then grumbled, "He'd better be paying you double-time."

She reached up and kissed him on the cheek. "But of course."

The sheriff's dark brown gaze returned to Ty and just as he started to speak again, Evan said, "Why don't you follow Dad to town in your rental car, Ty. That way you can collect your stuff and be on your way."

Her father's lips tilted in a calculated smile. "I don't mind taking Ty to town. As a matter of fact, I insist. Gotta come back out this way later anyway, so I can drop him off."

I'm sure he'll love driving me to town, Ty thought as he grabbed his shirt from the sofa and headed for the bathroom. *Just what I need...an angry, overprotective father drilling me about my intentions with his daughter all the way to the station.*

4

"What are your intentions with my daughter?" Jake said as soon as they started down the drive toward the main road.

Ty caught himself before he sighed out loud. "Pardon?"

"You heard me," the man grunted.

Ty narrowed his gaze. "I'm just here for my sister's wedding, Sheriff."

"Evan's a virgin," Jake said as if he hadn't spoken.

When Ty didn't respond, he continued in a gruff tone, "I don't like that you don't seem surprised by my statement. She is *still* a virgin, isn't she? She damn well better be, Hudson."

"And just why the hell is Evan's sex life or lack thereof anyone's business?" Ty snapped, more than a little annoyed for Evan's sake. Obviously he wasn't the only guy the sheriff had shared this information with.

"Because she's my little girl," the sheriff countered as if that answered everything.

"What Evan chooses to do or not do is up to her and no one else."

Jake's dark eyebrows drew together. "You've got some brass ones. I'll give you that. Mine are bigger. Her mother died when Evan was ten. She's all I've got, and no one is going to screw with her, either literally or figuratively. Am I making myself clear?"

"Perfectly," Ty said in a terse tone as he peered out the window. Why did he even say anything? It wasn't like he was going to take Evan up on her proposition. But for some reason, the fact the whole damn town was probably aware of her virginity bugged the shit out of him. No wonder she wanted to get rid of it. It'd become a thorn in her side, instead of something special to save for the right man in her life. With an overbearing father like the sheriff, he knew exactly why Evan was still a virgin. In such a small town, no one would go against the man without putting a ring on her finger.

Well, no one, except me, he mentally finished, even though he never planned to act on it.

"HEY, BIG BROTHER," Jena said as she hugged him. Ty gave her a bear hug and twirled her around. He didn't realize how much he'd miss seeing his sister until she moved to Texas a couple of months ago.

"It's great to see you, too." Setting Jena on the ground he looped his arm across her shoulders as he shook Harm's outstretched hand. "Good to see you again, Harm. You ready to make an honest woman of my sister?"

"Ty! We waited for *you*." Jena jabbed him in the ribs with her elbow then moved over to hug Harm's waist.

Harm kissed her on the temple and pulled her close, a wide grin on his face. "Hell yeah, I'm ready," he replied as he tilted his Stetson back.

"What took you so long to get here this morning? You said you'd be here bright and early."

Ty took in his sister's rosy cheeks, the highlights in her blonde hair lightened even more by the Texas sun. She was truly happy. His gut tightened a little at the thought she'd be permanently so far away. He'd just have to make an effort to visit her a couple of times a year.

"The sheriff showed up this morning to let me know my rental car had been recovered along with my stuff."

Jena frowned. "I'm sorry about your car getting stolen. What rotten luck."

"Yeah, Texas seems to do that to me," he said in a wry tone.

"Well, I'm glad you're settled at the Double D. At least you'll have the privacy you like so much," she teased.

"You said Ty could stay at your aunt's house?" A concerned expression crossed Harm's face.

Jena glanced at her fiancé. "Yes, why?"

Harm gave her a sheepish look, "'Cause I told Evan she could use the house while she was taking care of Flash."

"Oh." Jena's worried gaze jerked to her brother, then back to Harm.

Ty smiled. "Don't worry. We've worked it out. Evan owes you a lamp, but other than that..."

Confusion replaced the worry in his sister's gaze. "A lamp? Do I want to know?"

"Not really." He gave a half-laugh. "I'm only here for the wedding so it's not a big deal."

"But there's only one bed."

"There's also a couch," Ty reminded his sister.

Harm suddenly grinned, then raised his eyebrows. "Oh yeah, the couch. Remember that night—"

Jena elbowed him, blushing bright red. "Okaaaaay, that's enough." Casting her gaze back to Ty, she continued, "I'm convinced. As long as you and Evan are okay with it."

Ty had never seen his sister so flustered. She really had fallen in love with Harm. And the way Harm looked at his sister, like the sun rose and set with her...if Ty had questioned their whirlwind romance before, he didn't now. Good for them. Hopefully that meant this marriage would last. God knew enough of them didn't. Shoving his hands in his jeans' pockets, he rocked on his heels. "No problem. So what are the plans for the next couple of days?"

LATER THAT DAY, Ty had just rounded the bend up the long drive toward the Double D when he saw Evan trying to hold a yellow lab by its scruff while she pulled the garden hose toward the muddy dog. The dog ducked out of her hold and back away, wary brown eyes darting to the water pouring out of the hose.

"You're a lab, Daisy, you're *supposed* to love the water," she cajoled as she reached for the animal once more. When the dog dodged her hand again and took a couple more steps back,

Evan glanced over her shoulder and called to Ty, "Don't just sit there. Come help a lady in distress."

Climbing out of his car, Ty approached with a grin. "Apparently, the *lady* doesn't want a bath."

"Har, har, very funny," Evan said, wrinkling her nose. "Daisy's hurt, but I can't tell what's going on or tend to her wound with all this mud caked on her." She gestured to the antsy dog. "If you can just hold her by the scruff so I can get her cleaned up, I would appreciate it."

"With no collar to ID her, how do you even know this *is* Daisy?" he asked, taking a step toward the dog. As he reached for the dog's scruff, the animal froze and began to shake all over. Ty cast Evan a "what'd I do" look.

She nodded toward the dog. "You just confirmed it for sure. Daisy's terrified of men for some reason. She's owned by Agnes—a neighbor who lives a few acres over."

"Hey, Daisy," Ty said as gently as he could, but as soon as he reached for her once more, the skittish dog ran over to Evan's side to lean against her jean-covered thigh.

Ty gave a wry smile. "Guess water is the lesser of two evils."

"Would you mind?" Evan asked, lifting the hose toward him, while she grabbed onto Daisy's scruff.

Taking the garden hose, Ty nodded toward his shampoo travel bottle Evan had brought outside. "Think Daisy's going to like eau de men?"

Evan laughed. "I just grabbed the first thing I could once I saw what a mess she was." Pouring the shampoo across Daisy's coat, she spoke to the dog, "Well, girl this is one way for you to get used to guys...smelling all masculine."

Once Evan had bathed the dog all over, Ty turned the

sprayer on the hose to low, then began to wash the suds away to uncover Daisy's beige fur. "How'd she end up here?" he asked as he took extra care with the spray around an apparent wound on the dog's leg.

Evan rubbed the fur across Daisy's back, making sure all the soap was gone. "I'd just turned into the driveway when I saw Daisy loping across, heading toward the house. My guess is she must've tugged right out of her collar and leash, then took off for the creek. Agnes always keeps a collar on her."

Ty nodded to the gash on Daisy's left leg. "That wound looks deep. No wonder she was limping."

After Ty turned off the hose, Evan gently lifted Daisy's leg to inspect the wound. "You cut yourself good, didn't you, girl?"

Daisy whimpered, then licked Evan full on the mouth. Ty held back a laugh at Evan's expression; *ugh* tempered with love. It was an adorable combination.

"You're right, it's fairly deep." Evan turned apologetic eyes his way. "I'm sorry to ask for another favor, but would you mind rubbing Daisy down with a towel and sitting with her while I run home to get my other first aid kit? The one I keep in my car doesn't have all the things I'll need to treat this wound."

"No problem," Ty grabbed the folded towel, then moved to sit on the porch steps. Evan tugged a reluctant Daisy over to Ty's side and waited until he had a good grip on the dog's scruff before stepping away.

As Daisy began to shake uncontrollably under his tight hold, Ty shook his head. "She really doesn't like guys, does she?"

Evan backed toward her car with a shrug. "Agnes told me she got her as an adult at a shelter a couple years ago. Daisy was probably mistreated by a man in the past, so be gentle with her. I'll be right back."

Patting Daisy's quivering head, Ty waved her on. "We'll be fine. See you in a few."

EVAN DROVE to her office as quickly as she could. It probably would've been easier to bring Daisy here, but she had a feeling Ty would've insisted on helping, and the last thing she wanted was for him to see *Evan Masters, DVM* plastered across the office front door.

Grabbing her black bag, she filled it with all the supplies she'd need to take care of Daisy's wound, then headed back out the door, and right into Chad. At six feet four and built like a linebacker, running into him felt like she'd hit a solid oak door. Evan stumbled back.

"There you are! I've been looking for you," Chad said with a big grin, his blue eyes pleased as he clasped her arms to steady her.

Sitting in your truck, waiting for me to come home takes "looking for me" to a whole new level. Evan resisted the urge to roll her eyes. Instead, she pushed past him, "Sorry, can't talk, Chad." Holding up the black bag, she continued. "I've got a patient waiting for me."

Chad gestured to her door as she rounded the front of her car. 'That's what your office is for. Anyway, isn't today supposed to be your day off?"

Evan snorted. "Can you imagine bringing livestock in for an office visit?"

Chad huffed his frustration. "I waited for you at your house last night." He frowned. "But you never showed."

"I was out 'til after midnight, delivering a foal for Charlie," Evan said, then climbed into her SUV.

As she drove off, she saw Chad's gaze narrow after her car.

Her hands tightened on the steering wheel. Great. She didn't need Chad's interest suddenly peaking to "annoying level". What would it take for him to learn that she wasn't interested?

When Evan drove up to the house, but didn't see Ty or Daisy, unease rippled through her. *Where could they be?* Carrying her bag, she walked around the side of the house, then checked out back. Nothing. After she checked the barn, there was only one place left to check.

As she rounded the other side of the house and started to cut across the front yard, Evan paused when she heard Ty's deep timbre floating through the open kitchen window.

The slow, steady intonation in his voice told her he was reading out loud. Evan tilted her head to listen. He was reading the article about the Tanner brothers' rodeo ranch that had run in their local newspaper yesterday. Ty paused reading for a second to say, "This article doesn't say it, but the Tanners are my cousins. Now you have the inside scoop."

Dying of curiosity, Evan tip-toed across the front porch and peeked in through the kitchen window. What she saw hit a major "awww" meter. Ty was sitting on the couch, reading from the newspaper, while he rubbed his hand along Daisy's back. Daisy was resting her chin on his thigh, her big brown eyes staring up at Ty in total adoration.

Ty trailed off as Evan walked through the front door. "I see you got Daisy to calm down," Evan teased.

Ty laid the paper on the table next to the couch, but kept his hand on Daisy's back to keep her from jumping down to get to Evan. "Stay," he quietly ordered, then turned a sheepish grin Evan's way.

"My business partner called to discuss work and while I was talking with him on the phone," Daisy settled down. When I hung up, I realized she was reacting to my voice, or a steady stream of words, so," he glanced at the paper. "That's how I got her in here and up on the couch."

Setting her black bag down, Evan kneeled in front of Daisy. "You've got Ty's number, don't you?" she said with a wink as she rubbed Daisy's head.

When she opened her bag, Ty leaned forward to glance into her bag. "Can I help?"

As Evan glanced back down at her bag, her initials, etched in gold on the black leather (it was a gift from her father when she graduated from vet school), jumped out at her. Nudging the bag tight against the couch to hide the monogram, she took out a towel, shaving clippers and then various other medical supplies she'd need to numb then suture Daisy's wound and smiled at Ty. "Just rub her back and keep doing what you're doing." She cut her gaze to Daisy, who was still staring at Ty. "She's apparently mesmerized by your voice."

While she shaved away a section of fur around Daisy's wound, Evan said, "You mentioned a business partner. What type of business are you in?"

"I'm a part owner in an architectural firm."

"Ah, business minded *and* creative. What made you decide to be an architect?" she asked as she cleaned her hands, then pulled on some gloves.

Ty's gaze tracked her every move as he answered, "Ever

since I was a kid, I've always built elaborate structures." A wry smile. "My parents couldn't buy enough Legos. My collection got kind of out of control."

Nodding, Evan smiled while she readied the gauze, alcohol swab, shot of numbing medicine and needle. "I know exactly what you mean. I was always bringing home an injured animal, constantly nursing them back to health, so becoming a —" she caught herself before she said vet and kept her focus on Daisy's wound until she'd stitched the entire wound."

As soon as she clipped the last knot, Ty asked, "Becoming a..."

Evan glanced up at him. "Oh, a vet's assistant. It seemed like a natural progression for me."

He nodded toward the sutures she was wrapping with gauze. "You just sewed Daisy up like a pro. I hope that vet is paying you what you're worth."

Evan laughed as she taped the end of the gauze down. "I'm always hearing that the practice couldn't run without me."

Ty grunted. "Well, at least he acknowledges your worth."

Once she'd removed her gloves, Evan sat on the couch and rubbed Daisy's back. "I'm curious. How did you know your partnership would work? That seems like a big leap, going into business with someone."

Ty patted Daisy's head, then rubbed her ears. "Peter and I were roommates in college. When you're in the same Fraternity and the same major, you get to know that person very well." Running his hand across Daisy's back, Ty shrugged. "Pete's the brother I never had. If I were suddenly unable to work, I'd trust him to run the business for me until I could get back on my feet, no matter how long it took."

"Wow, I couldn't imagine trusting someone that much.

Peter must be one heck of a guy," Evan said as she slid her hand absently along Daisy's back. Ty came across as the type of man used to giving orders, not taking them. That he trusted Peter so much said a lot about his friend's character. Evan had been independent from the time she could take two steps. Other than her father—whom she'd never go into business with, the man did *not* have a head for numbers—she'd never been close enough to anyone to want to seek their counsel or ask for their help. She'd shouldered all the responsibility for her business from the get go.

Ty's hand landed on hers, drawing her out of her musings. "Just like everything else worthwhile in life, Evan, trust is earned."

As his gaze searched hers, Evan felt like he was talking about something else, something more than his partnership with an old friend.

Daisy began to squirm under their hands and Evan quickly stood, saying, "Thanks for the advice."

As Ty stood, Evan retrieved a spare leash from her bag. Looping it loosely around the dog's neck, she said, "I need to take Daisy home. I called Agnes own my way back to the house. She was so relieved that Daisy was okay. Daisy's all she's got, since her husband passed away a couple years ago. I'm sure she'll be waiting by her door with the treat box in hand."

Leading Daisy to the door, she smiled. "Thanks for your help, Ty. And Daisy thanks you too."

Right on cue, Daisy barked, making Ty and Evan laugh.

Ty GRABBED a shower after Evan left, glad to be finally rinsing off a long day's grime. He'd hung with his sister and Harm all day, helping with chores on their ranch. His shoulders ached from all the bales of hay he'd helped lift. Even though he exercised regularly, he'd used muscles today that he didn't necessarily exert on a regular basis. He'd forgotten how good it felt to work on a ranch.

Before he'd left the ranch, he'd ignored the heat and taken a long ride on one of Harm's stallions. Damn, that was an awesome rush. It'd been a long time since he'd felt so free, galloping in the hot wind on the open range.

He'd have stayed out longer, but Jena and Harm needed to get ready, since they were hosting their long overdue engagement party tonight. Jena had waited to have it until Ty could attend. He was glad it was at one of the local bars, a fun, very casual place called Rockin' Joe's.

As the warm water slid down his body, Ty's mind wandered to Evan. What had she done today before he'd seen her with Daisy? He'd been surprised and impressed with Evan's quick, efficient medical skills and her general easy way with animals. She was a natural.

He might not have any plans to seduce her, but the feel of her hand under his just now had ignited avid interest within him. He couldn't help but remember how her sweet body felt pressed against his this morning. When he closed his eyes under the hot spray pounding on his head, he still smelled her vanilla and cinnamon scent. He pictured her naked and wet... like she'd been yesterday. But this time she was in the shower with him. He'd pull her close and inhale the soft skin along her neck, then kiss the sensitive spot where her shoulder met her throat.

She'd moan and his balls would tighten at the sexy sound.

His erection hardened instantly at the turn in his train of thought.

Ty placed a hand on the shower wall while he grasped his hard erection. He imagined how good Evan would feel pressed against him, how warm and wet. She'd feel like the perfect fit when he slid inside her. He gritted his teeth at the sensations his mind conjured as he stroked his length. As much as he preferred women with lots of experience in bed, Evan's innocence, combined with her guileless nature, attracted him on so many levels, while her obvious independence intrigued him.

His lower stomach muscles tightened as he came close to peak. Ty took deep breaths to halt his climax just before he came. Damn, the anticipation felt good. Focused concentration and flexing his lower muscles worked every time. His shoulder and chest muscles relaxed as he gripped himself once more.

A cool breeze hitting his wet skin caused his eyes to snap open. He turned in time to see the shower curtain fall back into place. Through the frosty material he made out Evan's form exiting the bathroom.

His chest instantly tightened in sexual response. Damn, she'd been watching him. Unabashed curiosity and innocence...what a fucking erotic combination! The thought caused his erection to fill full of blood, harder than it had been, while his balls pulled tight in heightened anticipation.

He imagined pressing Evan against the shower wall, cupping her sweet ass and lifting her so he could bury himself in her warm sheath. Ty grasped his cock tighter. As he slammed his fist straight to the base, he let go of the physical control he'd been holding back. He groaned, jerking his hips through the explosive climax ricocheting through him in long, hard bursts.

As his movements slowed, Ty knew that if he'd had Evan in the shower with him right then, he would've relished every sensation; from the hot water pounding on them, to the feel of her soft skin pressed against his, to her vanilla and cinnamon smell. The sound of her moans mixed with his while their soap-coated bodies slid against each other would be an incredibly visceral experience.

Too damn bad he didn't plan to go there.

5

Evan's face flushed as she exited the bathroom, not in embarrassment, but in sheer sexual excitement. She'd watched the water sluice over Ty's broad shoulders and down his cut chest and abs. Her gaze had locked on his hand around his erection. The man not only had a body to die for, but he was also exceptionally well-endowed. She might be a virgin, but growing up a tomboy and hanging with guys just being guys, she'd seen enough to know the difference.

As she left the house and headed for the barn, her mind replayed the scene she'd just witnessed. Watching Ty slide his hand down his erection, taking himself to the edge only to expend mental and physical effort to hold back his orgasm, was the most sensual sight she'd ever witnessed. What had possessed her to peek, she had no clue. Ty was like a magnificent stallion, and she couldn't resist checking out all his fine lines. Before he opened his eyes, she left as quickly as she could. Thank God. She didn't know what she would've said or done if he'd caught her standing there watching him.

When she entered the stall, Flash danced around, excited to see her. Evan checked the horse's leg, then patted her neck and whispered in her ear, "You're antsy, aren't ya, girl?" This time she left the bandage off. Flash was better today. Maybe some fresh air would do the horse some good. Evan knew she could certainly benefit from it.

After she'd saddled Flash, Evan took her out in the pasture behind the barn where the mare quickly moved from a walk to a trot. Flash had been cooped up in the stall in the final stages of healing from her leg injury for the past couple of days. Up until today, Evan had allowed the healing horse short walks, but she felt Flash was ready and antsy for more.

As the wind blew through her hair and her body rocked with the horse's movements, her thoughts turned to the arousing scenario she'd just witnessed with Ty. Her heart raced and her body began to ache as sexual frustration welled within her.

EVAN ARRIVED AT ROCKIN' Joe's just after eight. Harm and Jena's engagement party had started at seven. Go figure, she was always late. But people had come to expect that of her. The nature of her job had her on constant on-call status.

Harm and Jena had rented out the entire place, so everyone there was an invited guest. She was glad they'd decided to have their engagement party in a casual atmosphere like Rockin' Joe's. She tugged at the hem of her baby pink tank top and straightened her silver and turquoise belt buckle at the waist of her jeans as she glanced around the crowded bar. Since her mother died when she was young, Evan grew into adulthood with men as her only influence. Needless to say, that left her with a wardrobe full of jeans, tank tops, T-shirts, boots and little else.

To Evan, being "dressed to kill" meant she wore her hair down, and her shiny boots, not her scuffed ones. She glanced down at the scuffed boots on her feet with a wry smile. Her hair fell toward her face with her movements. Lifting her head, she tossed the strawberry-blonde loose waves away from her face with a sigh. At least she wore her hair down tonight.

Her dad and uncle were talking to Harm and Jena next to the bar. She'd catch up with them later when she gave Harm an update on Flash.

She waved to Colt Tanner and his brothers Mace and Cade, who were standing near a corner booth drinking beers. Cade must've come home briefly from his rodeo touring, she thought with a grin as Mace picked up a beer from the table. He made his way over to her and handed her the longneck.

"How's it going, Evan?" he asked over the loud country music.

Evan took the beer and met Mace's hazel-green gaze. The man had one of the most engaging smiles she'd ever seen. He always knew how to make a person feel welcome and, if that person happened to be a female, definitely appreciated.

"What's the beer for?"

He laughed, glancing at his watch. "I knew you'd be late, 'bout an hour. Thought I'd have a drink ready for you when you got here so you could catch up with the rest of us."

"Thanks for keeping me up to speed." Evan grinned as she took a sip of her beer.

Out of the corner of her eye, Evan spied Chad shouldering through the crowd. He was making his way toward her, a determined look on his face. Her heart jerked and her stomach tensed. She didn't want to deal with him tonight. Grabbing Mace's hand, she said in a bright voice, "Come on, let's dance."

Mace followed her line of sight, then tugged her along. "He hounding ya?"

"Like a dog after his favorite bone." She rolled her eyes and followed him to the dance floor, her boot heels making pleasant thuds on the wood underneath her.

Mace took her beer and set it on a table before they stepped into the dance floor area. Garth Brooks' "Rodeo" was blaring from the speakers and Evan teased Mace as he pulled her against his hard chest. "I should be dancing this song with Cade."

He flashed her a devil-may-care smile. "Cade's not the dancing sort, darlin'. You know I'm a helluva lot more fun."

Evan laughed at Mace's self-confident comment as they began to dance. He always made her smile.

"Evan." Chad's voice sounded behind them. She tensed and missed a step, almost stomping on Mace's foot.

"She's dancin' at the moment." Mace gave him a direct, penetrating look.

"I'm talking to Evan, not you," Chad glared at Mace.

Evan felt Mace's shoulders tighten underneath her fingers. She glanced at Chad. "Chad, as Mace said, I'm dancing right now."

Chad's hand landed on her shoulder. He turned her to face him. "Not anymore you're not. We need to talk."

Mace grabbed Chad's upper arm. His expression turning serious. "I think you need to take a break, champ."

"Get the hell off me," Chad said, shrugging Mace's hand off his arm.

Running his hand through his short hair, Chad cut a frustrated gaze back to Evan. "Where *were* you last night?"

"I told you, working."

Hard lines formed around his mouth. "Charlie said you left his place around nine."

He was checking up on her? This was ridiculous and embarrassing. "You had no right to ask Charlie anything about me."

Chad scowled. "I've tried to talk to you, but you're never around."

Evan felt several pairs of eyes turn their way. People had stopped dancing around them. Damn, Chad was making a scene. She didn't want to spoil Harm and Jena's party. Maybe if she just walked outside to talk to him, he'd leave her alone.

Stepping out of Mace's arms, she started to say, "Let's go outside, Chad..."

At that moment, Ty stepped next to Mace and spoke in a calm tone, "I believe the lady said what she had to say."

"Who the hell are you?" Chad all but yelled at Ty.

"I'm the man she was with last night," Ty replied. His green gaze zeroed on Chad, daring him to say another word.

Evan's cheeks flooded with color as a hush spread throughout the crowd. Even the music had stopped...or had the song just ended? God, she hoped the music was just segueing into a new song.

Shock crossed Chad's face, then sheer fury replaced his surprised expression. "She's mine," he growled as he took a swing at Ty.

Evan blinked when she realized Chad was the one suddenly lying facedown on the floor. Ty had moved so quickly and with such fluid movements, he'd disabled Chad, bending his arm back, in less time than it took for her to glance his way in surprise.

Heavy boot heels stomped across the wooden dance floor. "Do I need to get involved?" the sheriff's voice boomed near them.

Ty glanced up at her father, then back down at Chad as he released him. "No, I think he was just leaving."

Chad scrambled to his feet. "I want you to arrest him for assault." He scowled as he rubbed his shoulder.

Jake narrowed his gaze on Chad. "You'd better leave before I forget I'm the sheriff and follow my *fatherly* instincts."

Chad met his own father's gaze as the mayor walked up behind the sheriff.

"Dad?"

The tall man nodded his silver head. "Go on, son. No need to spoil Harm and Jena's evening."

"I still want to talk to you," Chad said to Evan before he turned on his boot heel and left the bar.

Her father gave Ty a curt nod, then focused his gaze on Evan. "Until we put a security system in your house, you shouldn't leave your home unattended at night."

His comment came across loud and clear. He didn't want her staying at the ranch house. Period.

Evan lifted her chin a notch. No one told her what to do. Not even her father.

Another song had just started up and before she could comment, Ty took her hand. "I believe you said I owe you a dance."

Evan's gaze darted between Ty and her father. She felt a need to assert her independence from *all* men, but the thought of being held close to Ty offered major appeal. She glanced at

Mace, who winked and said, "You should grant your rescuer at least one dance."

Her father grunted, but didn't say a word before he turned away. The crowd around them had begun to dance once more. As Mace walked away, Ty wrapped his arms around her waist and pulled her flush against his hard chest. Evan closed her eyes for a second and relished the sensation of being surrounded by Ty's strength, his heat and his seductive smell.

Sighing her approval, her gaze landed on his open-necked, button-down shirt. Today he looked very much "the cowboy" with his jeans, chambray shirt and boots. If it weren't for his Maryland accent, she could easily mistake Ty for a Texas cowboy, born and bred. It was the way he carried himself. He exuded sheer masculine confidence in every movement he made.

"I don't know if I should punch you or kiss you for what you did. Either way, thanks," she whispered in his ear. The man had gone up against her father. That took some big *cojones*.

"Chad's a prick," he commented, his breath warm against her neck.

Evan closed her eyes once more and imagined that Ty wanted to hold her in his arms, instead of the fact he'd asked her to dance to head off an argument between her father and her and probably to keep the peace for Harm and Jena. Why did Ty have to have some stupid rule against sleeping with virgins?

She remembered the shower water sluicing over his gorgeous, naked body and the sight of him in full arousal. The thought made her shiver. Of course, her desire probably had to do with the fact the man also really knew how to dance. He matched her movements, step for step, making sure to keep their bodies flush against one another. From his intense charisma to his natural rhythm, Ty made her feel sensual, needy and so incredibly turned on.

When his lips grazed her neck, she gasped in surprise and her eyes flew open, locking with his steady gaze.

His fingers tightened on her waist before he lowered his hands to her hips. Pulling her forward, he fit her body even closer to his. A serious expression had settled on his face. "I'll take the virginity you so willingly offered, but we're going to do it my way."

"Your way?" Her heart beat a rapid dance, hammering her chest. The thought of having Ty's naked body gliding against hers made her breasts ache and her lower stomach muscles tense in aroused anticipation.

His warm hands slid up her waist, then higher. He applied pressure on her back until her chest was pressed against his. His mouth hovered close, his gaze colliding with hers. A feral smile tilted his lips. "Yeah, *my* way. Those are the terms. What do you say?"

Unable to form a coherent response, Evan nodded her assent.

As soon as the song ended, Ty stepped away. "I'll see you back at the Double D."

Evan spent the rest of the evening going through the motions of socializing. Ty's agreement had left her body on a tightly wound spring. She was so aroused at the thought of being with the sexy man she thought for sure if someone touched her she'd go up in flames. Finally, after being at the party for a good hour and a half, she made her way over to Harm and Jena.

"Hey, you two. Nice party."

A look of concern crossed Jena's face. "You okay, Evan?"

Evan grimaced, then shrugged. "Sure. I'm sorry about the Chad scene."

Harm wrapped an arm around Jena's shoulders. "No need to apologize, Evan. Chad was way outta line."

"Yeah. I had no idea my brother knew martial arts. Speaking of which..." Jena paused as she glanced around the room. "Did he leave already?"

Harm nodded. "He told me he'd see us tomorrow at the ranch."

"You going to put him to work again?" Jena laughed, amusement reflected in her gaze as she looked up at her husband-to-be.

"Hell yeah. If I've got an extra hardworking hand at my disposal for a few days, I'm gonna soak it for all it's worth."

"He loves it." Jena laughed, then sobered. "Just make sure he's not too dog-tired to give me away at the wedding."

"Noted." Harm's dark brown gaze shifted to Evan. "If Flash is finally up to speed, I'll come get her tomorrow."

Evan slowly shook her head. "I'm not sure if she's ready to be out on the range by herself yet. I took her for a trot earlier today. She seemed to enjoy that. How about I'll bring her by Steele Way tomorrow and let her visit for an hour or so. Then I'll take her back for a couple more nights. I just want to be sure she's fully recovered. Babysitting an injured horse is the last thing you should be doing right now with all your wedding stuff going on."

Harm smiled his appreciation. Rubbing his jaw, he glanced at Jena. "It just occurred to me that Ty might want a horse while he's at the Double D. He really seemed to enjoy the ride he took today."

Evan grinned. "Tell you what. I'll bring Flash by tomorrow in my two-sided trailer. Then I can carry another horse back for Ty."

Jena's hand landed on her arm. "I'm really sorry about the mix-up, Evan. Harm didn't tell me he'd already given you permission to stay at my aunt's house."

Evan flashed a sheepish smile. "It's been a good way to avoid Chad. Well, at least it seemed like a good idea."

"I've a mind to un-invite him to the wedding." Harm didn't bother to hide his annoyance.

Jena gripped his arm. "You know your parents are friends with the mayor and his wife. There's no reason to cause tension. I'm sure Chad just had a few too many beers tonight. He'll be fine at the wedding."

Evan nodded, relieved that Jena had jumped in to calm Harm's temper. "I agree. I don't want to cause any more friction."

Harm gave a curt nod. "Fine. But if Chad so much as steps one foot out of line during the wedding, I'll personally kick his ass."

"I have no doubt you'll follow through, too," Evan replied with a chuckle. "Well, I've got a lot to do tomorrow. I'm heading out."

"Why don't you come to the rehearsal party?" Jena suggested. "Since the wedding and the reception will be held at our ranch, to appease my mom's need for formality, she's hosting a semiformal party at the Wilshire Hotel tomorrow night. If you can work it around your schedule, you're welcome to come."

"Are you sure? Isn't that typically a wedding party event?"

Jena laughed. "My mom's invited the world to this affair. You're more than welcome."

Evan knew Ty would be there. The idea of spending more time with the irresistible man made her stomach flutter. "Count me in then. Thanks for the invite."

With each step she took across the floor toward the bar's exit, Evan's excitement grew. Ty's words reverberated in her head, *I'll see you back at the Double D.*

THE HOUSE WAS dark as she drove up the long drive. Disappointment made her chest ache. Had she somehow missed Ty? But as soon as she pulled into a space in front of the house her car's lights landed on Ty leaning against the porch post...as if he were waiting for her.

Evan's heart raced and her stomach tensed. She'd been so confident when she'd told Ty she knew how to please herself, but would he find her inexperience with men a turnoff or lacking in some way?

She cut the engine and turned off the car's lights, dousing the house in darkness. After she'd shut her car door and started to approached the porch, she couldn't decide which was louder, the buzzing of night bugs or her own pulse racing in her ears.

Ty's arms were crossed as he leaned against the porch in a casual stance. When she stood on the step below him, he didn't move or say a word. But even in the moon's light, she saw the glitter of desire in his gaze as he raked it down her body.

"I won't make you any promises."

Her lower stomach muscles tensed at his curt, dark tone. "I don't expect any."

"My way."

"Fine." She lifted her chin a notch at the challenge in his gaze. It was as if he were goading her, trying to get her to cry off.

"Come here," he commanded in a low rumble.

Straightening her spine, Evan climbed the final step and stood in front of him.

He didn't move, didn't lower his arms. He just stared at her with his intense gaze. Yet she felt his heat and her body reacted to his closeness...even with the wall of control and folded arms he held between them.

The tense silence lingering between them was getting to her. Evan started to speak, to break the tension, but Ty chose that moment to lower his arms and take a step toward her. "What did he do to you?" he asked.

"What?" She took a step back.

"If Chad didn't have sex with you, how far did he get?" he grated out as he turned and took another step.

His action forced her to back toward the door if she wanted to keep her gaze locked with his. Why did she feel he was purposefully trying to rile her?

The toe of his boot landed between her feet on the floor-boards. He crowded her personal space, his broad shoulders making her feel small for someone who was used to being on even ground with most men. Or was it his dominant charisma that made her feel that way? The tension emanating from him caused her to take another step back, but this time her boot heel hit the front door.

Her heart raced while her stomach clenched at his question. "I don't see what Chad and I did has any relevance."

The moon's light behind him immersed Ty's face in shadows. He placed a hand on the door behind her, caging her in.

"Did he touch you, bring you to climax with his hand?" he continued in a husky tone.

Evan's heart raced at his relentless, intimate questions.

When she didn't respond, Ty lowered his face close to hers. "It doesn't matter. For the next couple of days, I'm going to be the only man on your mind, the only man you want sliding inside you."

There was something about the quiet certainty of his tone that made her anxious. It wasn't arrogance, but more an assured confidence that had her breath hitching in her throat. Could she handle what Ty was sure to throw her way?

"I'm going to push you to your limit, take you out of your comfort zone."

Her spine stiffened at his low threat. "How do you know I won't take you out of yours?"

White teeth flashed in the dark. She felt his feral smile like a tiger running his tongue along her shoulder, sampling his prey before he took his first, deep bite. "You're welcome to try."

It was now or never. She had to show him she was no one's wilting flower to be trampled on.

Evan grasped his package through his jeans then ran her fingers over his erection before cupping his full length.

His body tensed and she smiled at his hissing intake of air. "I'm ready."

Ty pried her fingers off his erection, lacing his hand with hers. Grasping her other hand, he pulled them up over her head and pressed her hands against the door behind her. "I said, my way."

"I heard you the first time," she said calmly, even as her heart galloped at the forceful warning in his tone. Did he think he was going to lead the entire time? She might be innocent in some ways, but she definitely had a mind of her own and she damned well planned to use it. "Kiss me," she demanded.

Ty dipped his head, but instead of kissing her, his lips grazed her jaw.

She gasped at the sensation of his five o'clock shadow rasping against her soft skin. When she tried to turn her mouth toward his, he moved on to her neck, gently nipping at her skin.

His hot breath bathed her neck as he kissed a trail to the hollow at the base of her throat. Evan moaned at the torture he seemed willing to put her through. "You're going in the wrong direction," she sing-songed.

"Shhh," he said before he kissed her chin.

Ty's mouth felt warm and moist and so damn sexy. How could he expect her to just stand there and take it?

When he kissed the corner near her mouth, she tried once more to capture his mouth with hers, but he grasped her lower lip between his teeth and held her still.

Evan panted at his need to establish the pace between them. It made her want to push his buttons, to shove him over the edge. Flicking her tongue out, she traced it along his upper lip.

Ty's fingers tightened around hers right before his mouth covered hers. His tongue glided against hers in one of the hottest kisses she'd ever experienced. Heat flooded from her breasts all the way down to her center.

Evan tried to pull her hands free in order to wrap her arms around him, but a low growl rumbled in his chest as he held her still. Other than his hands, lips and tongue, no other part of his body touched hers.

But, ohmigod, what he could do with those sexy lips and that seductive tongue. He delved deep in slow, methodical thrusts, exploring her mouth, teasing her tongue, making her ache to feel him inside her. Just. Like. That.

"Let me go. I want to touch you," she panted between kisses.

"No," Ty said before he pressed his mouth against hers, harder this time.

No? What the hell? Anger filled her and she bit down on his tongue, stopping their kiss. Releasing his tongue, she asked, "Aren't you going to touch me?"

Ty let go of her hands, then took a step away, his expression tense and hard.

"Tomorrow."

Tomorrow? Was this some kind of twisted mind game to him? He was only here for a few more days. His stiff stance and the harsh rise and fall of his chest told her he wanted to go further.

She narrowed her gaze. "Are you screwing with me?"

He shook his head. "I told you. We'll do this my way. You can back out at any time you want."

Evan clenched her jaw and resisted the urge to give him a piece of her mind. The man was determined to draw this out. Suffering sexual frustration was not her idea of fun. She'd had enough of that on her own.

Grabbing the doorknob behind her, she opened the door and huffed, "Your loss."

Ty WATCHED Evan stomp across the room, then close her bedroom door behind her. His balls ached like a motherfucker at the sight of her sweet ass swaying in her jeans. Every fiber in his body ached for him to chase her down and rip her clothes off. To go at it like two wild rabbits, just like she wanted.

But her virginity held him at bay. He wanted her so turned on, she'd be prepared and begging for it when he took her. Slow and controlled was the best way to handle Evan...even if she didn't see it that way.

Lying down on the couch, he groaned inwardly as he adjusted his aching cock in his jeans. Why did he seem to be in this perpetual mode of blue-ball arousal when it came to Evan? When he'd seen that jackass Chad demanding Evan's attention, something in him snapped. That had to explain getting involved and his surprising decision to ignore his personal rule against sleeping with virgins. All he knew was, sheer fury had swept through him. He'd had to work hard to concentrate on all he'd been taught in his aikido training. *Remain calm. Use your opponent's anger and force against him.*

He'd wanted to snap the fucker's arm.

When the air-conditioning turned off, the house grew achingly quiet. If he'd followed Evan's request, the small ranch house would be full of the sounds and smells of heart-pounding sex. He closed his eyes at that thought and his cock turned unbelievably hard. Ty gritted his teeth and tried breathing techniques to calm his raging libido.

Once his pulse stopped pounding in his ears, the sound of feminine moans permeated his consciousness. Ty jerked his gaze toward the bedroom door to see it was ajar. It must've popped open when the air-conditioning clicked off.

Another moan floated his way, this one deeper than the last. As if invisible, seductive fingers beckoned him, he stood and walked toward the door. He couldn't resist the arousing sound.

Ty paused outside her door then slowly pushed it wide open.

The sight before him shot a jolt of sheer stimulation straight to his crotch.

The moon's light from the side window spread across the bed, illuminating Evan's gorgeous long legs. She was lying on her back, her neck and spine arched as she thrust her fingers deep inside her channel. Her white tank top only accentuated the dark nipples jutting against the thin cotton.

Ty's balls began to throb. He clenched his fists by his sides and fought the desire to join her—desire that raced through him in sparks of fiery arousal. If he didn't know better, he'd swear she did it on purpose just to throw him over the edge.

But Evan seemed completely oblivious to his presence and her uninhibited responses to her own stimuli just made him want her more. When she climaxed and sighed, Ty started to close the door to give her privacy.

But the door chose that moment to squeak. *Well, fuck!*

Evan gasped and her eyes flew open. She grabbed the sheet and pulled it over herself as she sat up on her elbow.

Ty straightened his spine and gave an unapologetic look. "Now we're even." He shut the door quietly behind him.

Embarrassed heat stole up Evan's cheeks. She stared at

the closed door while her heart jerked and her body still ached for a more fulfilling release. Not only had Ty just watched her in a very personal moment, but the man apparently knew she'd witnessed him doing the same in the shower. As mortified as she was, a thought struck her—had he been as turned on as she was by the sight? She snorted in annoyance and lay down once more. Obviously not, since he'd walked away.

Pulling the covers up to her chin, she contemplated what it would take to get Ty to totally lose it. His control intrigued her, but at the same time his steely determination go slow infuriated her. All she wanted to do was jump his bones. She didn't want her first sexual experience to be on a timetable. She wanted it to be spontaneous, uninhibited and real.

6

Ty'd been working nonstop since dawn. He was glad he'd worn his boots for the work Harm threw his way. The late-morning sun beat down on him, growing hotter by the minute. He'd ditched his shirt an hour earlier and sweat now coated his skin as he stopped the tractor near the barn and jumped down.

He'd thrown himself full-throttle into work this morning for a reason. That reason was named Evan...or Eve, he thought with a smirk. The woman was the epitome of forbidden temptation, all wrapped up in a gorgeous five-foot-ten woman he wanted nothing more than to bury himself into. Last night was one of the longest nights of his life.

After today's chores he knew he'd ache all over, but work had always been his escape—that and aikido. Jena had looked at him differently this morning as if she were surprised to learn something about him she didn't know. He'd smiled in memory at the look he'd seen on his sister's face last night when he'd taken Chad down. He never did tell her about his martial arts abilities. For him, aikido was more than just a tool for keeping in shape. It helped him learn to focus, to get the hell over past issues in his life and move on.

Squinting against the bright sunlight, Ty asked Harm, "What else needs to be done?"

Harm pulled a cowboy hat off the hook on the wall in the stables and threw it to him. "Why don't you hitch the flatbed to the tractor and get Keith to help you load up a couple of bales of hay for the stables."

"Does that mean I'll be mucking, too?" Ty chuckled as he plunked the black Stetson on his head.

Harm flashed a wide smile. "I knew I was marrying into a smart family."

Ty just shook his head. "Good thing I brought a change of clothes."

Evan's SUV bumped and jostled over the gravel road as she drove up to Steele Way ranch. She hoped Flash would be okay. The horse *should* feel very cozy. Evan had had to line the trailer with hay in order to get the skittish animal to go near it. Once she got Flash inside, the horse seemed to settle. Harm had said Flash loved going places, so maybe it'd been the double trailer that freaked the mare a bit. Evan wasn't certain of the reason, but she was glad disguising the trailer as a stall did the trick.

Jena met her as she jumped out of her vehicle. "Hi, Evan." Jena's gaze traveled from Evan's newly cutoff jeans and cropped T-shirt to her broken-in cowboy boots.

She grinned when her blue gaze met Evan's. "Nice tan! I've only ever seen you in jeans. You should wear shorts more often. You've got the legs for them."

Evan was thankful she'd worn shorts as much as she could when she was at home working in the yard. "Thanks for the compliment," she said with a laugh before moving around the back of the trailer to open the latch.

Three ranch hands rushed forth, saying in unison, "Here, let us help ya with that, Evan."

"Then again..." Jena began in an amused whisper near Jena's ear as the cowboys elbowed each other to be the one to open the latch. "Look at the dent you're putting into the work the ranch hands will get done today."

As the three men shouldered their way past each other, trying to get the horse down, Evan chuckled. "Hmmm, maybe it's a good thing I only plan to be here for an hour to exercise Flash."

"You're still coming to the rehearsal party tonight, right?" Jena asked.

Evan nodded. "I wouldn't miss it." Grasping Flash's bridle, she said, "I thought I saw Ty's car. Is he here?"

Jena gave her a knowing grin. "Yeah, he's here working his butt off." A thoughtful expression crossed her face. "Which is kind of interesting to see him working so hard, because my brother has always hated Texas heat."

"Really?" Evan led Flash over to the gated area as Jena trailed along.

"Yeah, Ty really doesn't like Texas. When we came here to sell off my aunt's property a couple of months ago, he couldn't wait to get back home." She tilted her head, reminiscing. "Come to think of it, he'd seemed to enjoy visiting my aunt the couple of summers we spent with her as teens." She sighed and flipped her blonde hair over her shoulder. "But then he was almost an adult that last summer we spent here and I guess ranching bored him."

Evan opened the gate to the smaller pasture. She'd just pulled the bridle off Flash when she heard a tractor over near the stables. "Go enjoy a nice jaunt, girl," she said, patting the horse's neck.

"Speak of the devil..." Jena said, drawing Evan's attention to her line of sight.

Evan's heart rammed at the sight of Ty's muscular back flexing as he and another guy rolled a bale of hay off the trailer next to the stables.

Ty happened to turn at that moment and his gaze locked with hers. Evan thought for sure her heart had stopped beating for a second or two. What was it about this man that enraptured her so?

His gloved hand touched the rim of his cowboy hat, while his gaze traveled to her exposed waist and legs before meeting hers once more. A slow, sexy smile formed on his lips, making her stomach tumble.

Evan couldn't stop from trailing her gaze over Ty's well-formed body. He had the perfect triangular shape. Broad shoulders and a trim waist. A thin line of dark hair started at his belly button and narrowed past his buckle into his jeans. Beyond his washboard stomach, he was so fit, he even had those mouthwatering defined muscles that dipped past the waistline of his jeans, splitting his lower belly into three perfect sections of cut muscles. Her fingers itched to run along his chiseled physique, to feel the hard flesh flexing against her.

"It's a good thing my brother has been working his ass off,

'cause now he isn't going to get jack done." Jena chuckled next to her.

Jena's comment jerked her out of her fantasy. "Don't worry. I won't keep Ty from working."

Jena grinned. "I was just teasing you. Ty's here for my wedding and a bit of vacation time. I would love to see him enjoy Texas again. Then maybe he'd visit me more than for my wedding."

The sad tone in Jena's voice caught Evan's attention. She hoped Ty enjoyed his stay, too. That meant he might come back for a visit in the future. *Don't even go there, girl.*

"Hmmm, maybe you should come by the ranch more often. I've never seen the men so...motivated," Jena mused, glancing at the three guys who were in the process of cleaning out the trailer's floor for Evan.

ONCE HE'D ACKNOWLEDGED EVAN, Ty refocused on the work. Harm must've been yanking his chain because the stalls had already been mucked. Fortunately, all he had to do was fill them with fresh hay.

As he moved back to the broken bale, he and Evan met face to face, their pitchforks digging in at the same time.

"Hey," she said in a low, husky voice.

Ty's groin instantly hardened when his gaze slid past her rosy cheeks to the cleavage the vee in her T-shirt allowed as she bent to retrieve a forkful of hay for her trailer. She'd pulled her hair back into a ponytail and ringlets had escaped the band to frame her face in light, sweaty curls.

He glanced at the trailer she'd been working to fill with fresh hay. "Need some help?"

She lifted the scoopful of hay and turned away, calling over her shoulder, "No thanks. I'm almost done."

Ty watched as she walked up the trailer's incline. When she dropped the hay, then bent slightly to spread it with the pitchfork, he almost choked as swift arousal slammed into his gut.

Her cutoff shorts rode her rear, giving him a perfect view of her ass while making him want to see the small private area the jeans material barely covered. He had no idea why the sight of those boots hugging her shapely legs turned him on, but damn...they did.

He swallowed and as he swiped his gloved hand across his sweaty brow, he noticed several ranch hands had stopped working and were staring in Evan's direction, totally mesmerized. Some were leaning against the fence, while others had paused mid-stride as they walked past.

When Evan leaned the pitchfork against the wall and dropped to her knees, preparing to spread the hay with her hands, biting jealousy gripped him. He knew the view the men were about to see. No fucking way were they getting that kind of show. Ty narrowed his gaze on the gawking group. "Is it lunchtime yet?"

His curt comment snapped the men back to attention. With last glances Evan's way, the men turned back to their work.

Ty grabbed his discarded shirt and shrugged into it as his boots ate up the distance between Evan and him. He mounted the metal ramp, ready to lay into her, but the sight of her sweet ass swaying as she moved around on her hands and knees caused the words to lodge in his throat.

Very little light filtered into the trailer. The roof and sides made the space feel hot and secluded as he moved deeper into the room. He didn't care if it smelled of horses. It was his own private haven with the woman who'd managed to steal his sleep and haunt his dreams.

The bits of hay Evan had dropped on her way up the ramp must've muffled his approach because Evan continued moving around, spreading the hay with quick actions as if she were oblivious to his presence. The lecherous part of him didn't want to end the show either, now that his body blocked anyone else's view.

As his heart rammed, his erection rubbed uncomfortably against his jeans. Ty adjusted himself, trying to relieve the pressure his button-fly caused. But touching himself only managed to turn him on more. Ty gritted his teeth, holding back his baser instinct to lean over and touch Evan. All he could think about was sliding his fingers along her inner thigh, listening to her breath catch as she waited for him find his way past the tiny crotch her jeans barely covered.

He heard her heavy breathing and though he knew it was from her exertions, he imagined she'd joined in his fantasy. He wanted her just like that too; breathless and sweaty and full of anticipation.

He closed his eyes, fighting his desire. But when he opened them and Evan actually wiggled her nicely rounded ass as she began to back up, he lost the battle.

Ty narrowed his gaze and squatted. With deliberate determination, he pulled off his gloves and tossed them to the floor. Resting his forearms on his knees, he sat and waited for Evan to back into him.

He literally felt a bone deep ache in his cock when she was within a foot of his reach. The moment she paused her backward momentum to grab something underneath the hay, Ty's patience had snapped. He moved forward, intending to clasp her curvy hips and pull her to him, when something hard hit him on the forehead.

Pain exploded in his head. "Sonofabitch!" he hissed as he fell onto his back and grabbed his brow above his right eye.

"Ohmigod, Ty!" Evan leaned over him, grabbing his hand. "I'm so sorry. I didn't know you were behind me."

"Apparently not," he said in a dry tone as he pulled his hand away. Bright red blood covered his palm. "What'd you hit me with? A shovel?"

Evan's brow furrowed as she looked at his cut. "No, Flash's bridle had fallen from the wall where I'd hung it earlier. It was underneath the hay. I was tossing it behind me to get it out of the way..." She paused, a perplexed look on her face. "Though I have no idea how I threw it so high it hit you in the forehead."

"I can think of better ways to get me flat on my back," he ground out.

She rolled her eyes and put out her hand, intending to pull him to his feet. "Come on. I have a feeling that cut will need stitches."

Ty shrugged off the pain and stood on his own. "Nah, I'll be fine."

A stubborn look crossed Evan's face. "You're going to the doctor, even if I have to hogtie you again to get you there. Grabbing his free hand, she shoved it toward his wound. Put your hand on your cut until I can get a bandage for you," she ordered before she ran down the ramp and disappeared.

Ty sighed and did as she asked, exiting the trailer behind her.

Evan met him as he came around the side of her SUV. "Okay, let me see it."

Once he lowered his hand, she quickly placed a bandage over his cut.

"Ow!" He winced and tried to pull back from the stinging pain.

Grabbing his arm, she was surprisingly strong as she applied pressure. "Hold still and stop being a baby. That has antiseptic in it that will disinfect your cut. Keep it on there while I drive you to the doctor."

Jena ran out of the house, taking the stairs two at a time, her gaze locked on the bandage on Ty's head. "What happened?"

"I whacked your brother with Flash's bridle by accident. Since the trailer's hooked to my SUV, can I borrow your truck to take him to Dr. Shelton's office?"

"Yes, of course." Jena clasped her brother's arm, worry lines on her forehead. "Are you okay?"

Ty started to roll his eyes, then winced. "I'm fine. I don't need to go to the doctor, you two."

Jena's lips set in a thin line. "If Evan says you need to see a doctor, then you'll go."

"She's just overreacting." Ty felt the women were definitely going overboard.

"Ty, Evan's a—"

"Um, we'd better get going," Evan quickly said, interrupting his sister.

"Yes, no point in arguing with him," Jena agreed. "I'll be right back with my keys."

When Jena returned with the keys, she said, "I'll drive."

Ty shook his head "You don't need to go. You need to get ready for your rehearsal."

"Are you sure?" Indecision reflected in his sister's concerned gaze.

Evan took the keys. "Positive. Ty's in good hands."

Jena cast thankful eyes Evan's way. "I know that for a fact. Thanks, Evan."

Once they'd climbed into Jena's vehicle, Evan drove straight to Dr. Shelton's office. As soon as she glanced at the truck's clock, she pressed harder on the pedal.

"Slow down, speedy. I'm not going to pass out on you."

"It's ten 'til twelve. Dr. Shelton closes at noon on Fridays."

Ty studied her. Yeah, they were short on time, but something else was bothering her. A few seconds ago, she was concerned, but she'd still joked and reprimanded him. Now she seemed tense.

Ty walked into Dr. Shelton's office behind Evan. While he filled out the paperwork, the doctor's secretary said, "Hi, Evan. It's good to see you. If you two will have a seat, Dr. Shelton will be out soon."

Ty and Evan had been sitting all of five minutes when a side door opened and a dark-haired woman in a long white physician's coat walked out.

"Ty Hudson. I can't believe it!" She looked up from her clipboard. Her surprised brown gaze locked with his.

Ty's chest constricted. He stood and worked hard not to show any emotion as he responded in a low tone, "Lily. It's been a long time."

Evan stood beside him. She glanced at him in curiosity, her gaze pinging between him in Lily, before addressing the doctor. "Hi, Lily. Ty needs stitches and probably a tetanus shot, too."

"Come on back." Lily smiled at him.

Ty's stomach soured as he began to follow her back to the exam room. Lily stopped when Evan joined him.

"You can wait out here, Evan. I can take it from here."

Ty glanced at Evan and noted the determined set of her lips. He could tell she was about to insist on coming back with them. "I'll be fine. Be right back."

The hurt look on her face pulled at his conscience, but Ty didn't want Evan to hear the mini-version of his past he was sure Lily would dredge up. Hell, *he* didn't want to hear it.

Once Evan walked back to sit down, Ty followed Lily through a door, down a hall until they reached an empty exam room on the left. His gaze ate up her petite, trim figure and her pitch-black hair clamped in a quick twist. She'd grown into the beautiful, sophisticated woman he'd thought she would become.

Lily closed the exam room door behind them. "Since I'll be working on your eyebrow, have a seat on the stool. When'd you last have a tetanus shot?"

"Six months ago."

She nodded and jotted down a note on his chart. "Since your last shot was fairly recent, I think you'll be fine without one."

Ty sat down on the cushioned rolling stool and waited.

"I couldn't believe it when I read your name on the patient's form." Lily washed and dried her hands then retrieved a bottle of astringent and cotton balls from the white cabinet with glass doors.

"Yeah, a real shocker," he commented. Floored was more

like it. The last thing he expected was for the town's doctor to be the woman he'd fallen in love with all those years ago. "I see you married." As he glanced at her name badge, her familiar jasmine scent invaded his senses. At least one thing about her hadn't changed.

"Soon to be divorced." A smirk curved her lips while she pulled on a pair of rubber gloves.

That comment surprised him. He started to raise his eyebrow but winced at the pain his action caused.

"Hold still." Lily dabbed at his wound with a cotton ball. Ty closed his eyes, blocking his view of her breasts, currently exposed by her v-neck cotton dress shirt under her open jacket. Once she'd cleaned the wound thoroughly, he felt her fingers manipulating his skin. "You have a nasty cut. Evan's right. You need stitches. Do you want painkiller?"

Ty shook his head. He wanted to remember the pain this woman caused him. Having her inflict him with physical pain would be a perfect reminder.

"How'd this happen?" she asked before returning to the cabinet.

"Got hit with a flying bridle." Ty watched her prepare the needle and thread.

Lily raised a perfectly arched eyebrow, casting an amused gaze his way. "That's not something one hears every day. Believe me, working here, I've heard it all." She turned away from the counter and approached with a scissors-type instrument. The end of the instrument was pinched closed, holding the needle and thread.

"I expected you to leave Boone. To seek that 'better life' you wanted." The comment came out before he could stop it. *Why the hell did he torture himself?*

She met his gaze with her steady chocolate brown one before she grasped his jaw and turned his head to the side so she could see better. "I got married. To a surgeon, no less."

"No surprise there," he grated out at the same time the needle pierced his skin above his eyebrow. Son of a bitch! Ty forced himself to ignore the stinging pain.

She pursed her lips at his sarcastic gibe, but continued to suture his wound. "Life doesn't always turn out as one plans. So what do you do now?"

Her tone might be conversational, but he felt the slight tug on the thread. No way was he telling her he was a successful architect. "A little of this and a little of that."

She chuckled. "So vague. You used to be such an open book. When I read Harm's wedding announcement in the paper and saw he was marrying your sister, I hoped you'd come back to Boone." Lily tied a knot and snipped the thread.

"Oh?" Her statement surprised the hell out of him.

Lily had finished her task, but she hadn't moved out of his personal space. "I never forgot about you."

Was that interest he heard in her voice? Ty's gut clenched. His pulse rushed in his ears, while Lily's words, spoken over two decades ago, came rushing back.

"Marry you? I don't want to be hemmed in by marriage. I want to make something of myself, Ty. To be someone important." He heard her voice as if it were yesterday. Each word had stabbed at his heart, shattering his image of true love. He'd loved her, damn it!

"You were the one who walked away," he reminded her in a cold tone.

Lily placed her hands on his cheeks. "We were seventeen, Ty. Too young to know what we wanted out of life."

"Did you find it?" he challenged, angrier then he'd ever been in his life.

Her gaze searched his as she moved her mouth closer to his. "Yeah, I think I just did."

Before her lips could connect, Ty grabbed her wrists and set her away from him. Releasing her, he stood. "Thank you for closing my wound." While she'd just mended one wound, she ripped open another—one that took a helluva lot more than stitches to close.

Seeing Lily again rekindled the devastating hurt she'd caused him all those years ago. Churning emotions he'd long buried, surfaced anew, tearing at his gut, making his stomach burn.

"Congratulations on the professional life you've created for yourself, Lily. I'm happy for you," he said before he opened the door and walked out.

"Let's go," Ty snarled as he walked out of the doctor's office.

Evan rushed to keep up with his long, determined strides. What was going on? Why did he seem angry? And here she thought she was the one all wound up. She hadn't meant to tense up earlier while on the way to the doctor, but when Jena almost spilled the beans about her, Evan panicked. She'd cut Jena off before she'd inadvertently told her brother that Evan was the town veterinarian. Evan wasn't quite ready to share that fact. Not yet. Maybe never, since he'd be leaving in a few days anyway. The less complications introduced into their budding—relationship? mutual agreement? Whatever was going on between them—the better.

"Lily got you all fixed up?" she asked, trying to lighten his mood. Evan's stomach had churned while she'd waited for Lily to take care of Ty's wound. Had Lily told him about her? Is that why he seemed distant, cold even?

"You could say that." He put his hand out for the keys. "I'll drive."

Evan met his deep green gaze, hoping to see some emotion, something to give her a clue as to what was going on in his head. He stared at her with an inscrutable expression.

As she dropped the keys into his hand, she stared at the stitches on his brow line. "I'm really sorry."

"No big deal." He wrapped his fingers around the keys, then opened the passenger side door for her.

They'd driven for a few minutes in silence when Ty finally spoke. "I don't think we're such a good idea."

"What'd you say?" she asked, her heart tightening.

Ty kept his gaze on the road. "I think it's best if we keep it platonic between us. Chad knows you're staying with me. That should be enough to keep him at bay."

His words hurt her more than they should have, considering nothing *had* actually happened between them. Yet Evan felt like he'd just grabbed her heart with both hands and twisted each half in opposite directions. Why did she have a feeling his change of heart had to do with Lily? She'd noticed how his demeanor changed from casual to alert the moment he saw her.

Evan might not have been socially adept growing up—being at least two years and in some cases, three years younger than her classmates in college, veterinarian and business school didn't help matters—but she'd never been one to hold back when she felt the need to speak her mind. And she wasn't about to start now.

"You're chicken."

"What the hell did you say?" His gaze cut her way, green eyes sparking in anger.

She crossed her arms. "You heard me. *Bock, bock.* What are you afraid of, Ty? That you might like it a little too much?"

Ty's jaw clenched. "You're awfully smug. For a virgin."

As much as his dig hurt her pride, she ignored his jab. "I didn't take you for the fowl type."

"I'll be gone day after tomorrow."

"All the more reason not to worry *you'll* get too attached." She met his narrowed gaze head-on, mentally daring him to come up with another excuse.

"The deal's off." He turned back to the road and tightened his fingers on the steering wheel.

We'll see about that. She stared out the window while sheer determination simmered, then rolled into a low boil inside her.

When they drove up Steele Way's main drive, Jena came out of the stables wiping her hands on her jeans. "How's your head?" she greeted her brother as he and Evan got out of her truck.

Ty dropped the truck's keys in her hand. "I'm as good as new." He didn't say a word to Evan before he walked off toward the stables.

As Evan came around the front side of the truck, Jena asked, "What caused that surly mood?"

Evan shrugged. "I was hoping you could tell me. He was fine until he went into the exam room. Then he came out in a mood after Lily stitched him up. I got the impression he knew Lily. Did he know Dr. Shelton?"

Jena's brow furrowed for a second. "Oh yeah. *That* Lily. Her married name threw me off. I'd forgotten about Ty dating Lily. The last summer we came to Texas, he and Lily spent a lot of time together. I hardly saw my brother those couple of months. That's why I ended up hanging with my cousins." She smiled. "The Tanner boys kept me busy dodging their teasing ways."

Evan's heart constricted to learn Ty and Lily had a past together, but that at least explained his mercurial change of mood. "Were they serious?"

Jena eyed her and a small smile formed on her lips. "Ah, I see where this is going."

Evan's stomach tensed. She needed to lighten Jena's serious thoughts. "You do? If so, I'd like to be in on the secret. Your brother will be gone in two days, Jena. I have no expectations other than to enjoy his company while he's here. I was just wondering why his mood went in the tank once he saw Lily."

As soon as Evan spoke, a sudden sinking realization hit her. Maybe the reason Ty called it off with her was because he decided he wanted to rekindle an old flame with Lily while he was here. The thought made her stomach cramp into tight, hard knots. She sighed as her own good spirits dropped.

Jena put her hand on Evan's shoulder. "I don't know what to say, Evan. My brother has always been pretty quiet when it comes to his relationships. He's not one to share much." A sympathetic look crossed her face. "Are you still going to come to the rehearsal party this evening?"

Evan straightened her spine. She'd gone this long without a guy. There was no reason to be concerned about a man she never had in the first place. "Absolutely. I'll be there. And I'll even wear a dress."

Jena smiled. "That's the spirit!"

Evan's gaze strayed to Ty as he came walking out of the stables with a bag of grain across his shoulders. He'd taken his shirt off again. The play of muscles across his chest made her stomach flutter. Damn, the man was built.

Evan shook her head to clear it. "I'd better collect Flash and a mount for Ty, then I'll head back. Tell Harm I'll keep Flash until the wedding is over. She should be back to her old self by then."

Jena smiled her appreciation. "Harm will be relieved to have her back. He doesn't like me riding the other horses as much. Says he trusts Flash's genteel nature when it comes to me."

"It's so obvious how much he loves you just by the way he looks at you, Jena."

Jena gave a soft laugh. "I'm just as much in love."

The adoration reflected in Jena's gaze as she glanced at her fiancé across the yard, solidified Evan's personal vow. Love like Harm's and Jena's existed. No matter how long it took, no matter how old she was, she refused to fall in love with a man who couldn't give her all his love in return.

7

Evan's emotions churned as she drove up to the small house she shared with Ty. After she'd loaded the horses and taken them to the Double D, she'd spent the last couple of hours at her office seeing clients who'd begged to be squeezed in on her "vacation" day. She didn't mind. Work helped her forget about Ty for a while. But as she parked her vehicle next to Ty's rental car, she couldn't help the tightening of her stomach or the way her breathing hitched at the idea of seeing the man again.

Her stomach rumbled, reminding her all she'd had to eat today was a bagel for breakfast. But the sensation of her heart hammering as she opened her car door and closed it behind her, overshadowed her need for food. She started toward the house when she heard one of the horses neighing in the stables.

Leaving her backpack beside her car's tire, Evan walked over to the stables. As she entered the small building, the sight of Ty grooming his horse made her pulse race. He faced away from her, giving her a perfect view of just how well his jeans hugged his rear.

The well-worn material cupped his butt cheeks and muscular thighs in such an inviting way, she wanted to walk up and run her hands down the soft material. The idea of worn denim over hard muscles pressing against her would be a major turn on. Or was it his broad, naked back she wanted to press herself against that got her motor going?

At this point, what did she have to lose? she told herself as she approached him from behind. He may like soft, petite women like Lily, but Evan was determined to show him what it was like to hold a woman who wasn't afraid to get her nails dirty.

When she was a step away, Ty paused his movements, holding the brush an inch above the horse's back.

He didn't turn to acknowledge her, but she knew he was aware of her presence.

His back tensed when she ran her fingers across his shoulder blades. Was that a rejection? She bit her lip and her stomach knotted. Her entire body stiffened, ready for his brush-off.

Evan almost pulled her hands away, but the play of tight muscles under her fingers was just too irresistible. Instead she moved her hands lower to cup those sexy muscles that ran around the front of his waist.

When she pressed her body against his back and started to move one of her hands toward his chest, Ty grabbed her wrist. "Evan—"

"Let me touch you." She planted a kiss on his warm skin.

Ty's grip on her hand tightened for a second then loosened. He moved both his hands to the horse's back, allowing her to continue her exploration.

Evan's fingers flexed across his pectorals. The thick muscles jumped under her fingers, making her smile. Despite his reservations, he enjoyed her touch.

She let go and quickly ducked underneath his arms until she stood between the horse and him, facing Ty. The long, thick bulge pressed against the fly of his jeans made her heart race. Her gaze locked with his forest green one. Bits of hay floated in the late afternoon sun streaming into the barn and Ty's musky smell mixed with the natural ones in the barn only enhanced her attraction.

They stood there, staring at one another for several long seconds. Her heart pounded at the intense look on his face and his clenched jaw.

Biting her bottom lip, she curled her fingers around his triceps then ran her palms up his shoulders. She stepped closer and moved her hands underneath his arms to trail her hands down his broad back. Evan thrilled at the heat emanating from him. She laid her cheek against his neck then kissed his tense jaw.

"I have no expectations, Ty. I know you'll be gone in a couple of days."

Ty didn't speak. Nor did he move to touch her. Frustration filled her, that he hadn't moved an inch. His body told her he wanted. Maybe she just needed to show him how much.

She kissed the pulse beating a rapid throb at his throat while her fingers moved to the button on his jeans.

Ty exhaled at the same time he turned his head, his stubbled jaw trapping her face against his throat. It was as if he couldn't stop himself. Her heart skipped a beat when she heard him inhale as if drinking in her scent in one long gulp of air. The thought made her stomach flip-flop and her body begin to throb.

He smelled so incredibly good, musky and spicy...of sandalwood, leather and sweat. She wanted to wallow in his scent, to spread it all over her.

They stood in the shade, but the sun slanted across the horse's back. As Evan pulled the buttons of his pants' fly apart. Ty stepped closer, purposely brushing his erection against her fingers.

Evan cupped the hard flesh through his fitted black cotton boxer briefs and the soft denim that still partially covered him. The man's impressive size made her sex flood with moisture.

She slid her hand inside his underwear and gripped the soft silky skin, fondling his erection. Rubbing her thumb across the tip of his cock, she stood on tiptoe and pressed her chest against his, whispering in his ear. "I don't know what made you change your mind, but are you sure you really want to?"

Before he could respond, Evan went back down on her heels at the same time she hooked her fingers in the waist of his jeans and jerked, pulling his pants down to his thighs. His muscular thighs stopped the jeans' descent any farther than his buttocks, but she'd achieved her goal. His erection sprang free. Her heart raced at the erotic sight of him standing at rigid attention. She wanted to trace every single well-defined vein, to discover what made him shudder with need.

Ty grabbed her wrist before she could touch him.

Evan's eyes flashed in anger. She was ready to argue, when Ty took her hand and cupped it around his cock.

Her heart leapt at his action. She elevated her gaze to Ty's heated one as he squeezed her fingers tight around him. His grip was so firm, when he slid her hand down his cock, she felt a steady thumping along its length.

"I feel your heartbeat." She didn't bother to hide the awe in her voice.

When he released her hand and refused to respond, she squeezed and used her hold to yank him closer. Damn the man and his controlled emotions!

Ty grunted when their bodies collided. The only sign she'd gotten to him was the slight flare of his nostrils. She wanted him involved and breathing hard. The man had yet to touch her. She knew he wanted her. Damn him.

She turned and kissed a path down his muscular chest and abs. As her mouth moved toward his erection, she hoped to elicit some kind of reaction.

Ty grabbed her ponytail, stopping her descent.

Frustration mounted. Why did the man block her every move? Evan's lips were a breath away from his hypersensitive skin. She was determined to win this round. Cupping his sac with her free hand, she blew across the plum tip in one long tantalizing exhale.

Ty's hips jerked forward at the same time she heard a low groan rumble in his chest.

He released her ponytail and Evan took advantage of her freedom. She encircled his erection with her lips, plunging his cock deep into the recesses of her mouth.

Ty's breathing changed as she began to slide her wet lips up and down the hard flesh. She sucked hard, locking her lips around him.

He speared his fingers in her bound hair, gripping the back of her head. Evan's heart raced when a low, ragged groan escaped his lips.

She ran her tongue in a slow, moist, decadent caress around his length like the red stripe winding its way up a peppermint stick.

Ty's erection grew even harder. He had to be close. Following her instincts, Evan tightened her lips and applied more arousing pressure, ready to take him over the edge, but Ty grabbed her shoulders and pulled her off him.

"Why—"

"My terms," he cut her off, a steely, determined look on his face.

Her heart leapt. At least he agreed to stick with their deal, but Evan didn't like that he still wanted to dictate the how and when of it.

She shrugged out of his hold, determined to have the last word. A knowing smile crossed her face before she turned to walk away, saying, "I'm a *lot* tighter than my mouth."

Before she'd taken a step, Ty grabbed her arm and yanked her close so his mouth rested against her temple. "I guarantee you, sweetheart, I'll feel a helluva lot bigger than your three fingers."

His intimate comment, spoken in a husky voice, sent heat shooting across her face. It had the desired effect. His promise both scared and excited her. Her thighs trembled when he released her, but she held her head high and forced one foot in front of the other as she walked out of the stables on unsteady legs.

Evan entered the cool house, wanting to scream at the stubborn man. She definitely needed a shower to wash away a long day of work—a cold one would probably be best. With a heavy sigh, she headed for the bedroom, gathered a change of clothes then walked into the bathroom. Once she'd turned the faucet on, she pulled her shirt off and leaned over to place her hand under the hard, pulsing water. It was almost the right temperature. Hot. Oh, yeah...she needed a cold one. She started to turn the faucet to cold when someone's hand came around her waist.

Evan let out a scream as Ty pulled her naked back against his bare chest. Without a word, he leaned over and shut off the shower.

Evan's hands shook as she laid them over Ty's hand around her waist. The sudden quiet in the room made her nerves tighten while she stood there half naked in his embrace. Her stomach tensed and her heart raced as she wondered what he had planned.

Before she could turn to face him, Ty scooped her up in his arms and carried her out of the bathroom. Evan's hands landed on his muscular shoulders as she gazed up at him.

Ty wasn't looking at her. He focused on the bed as he approached it. His boot heels ate up the low-pile carpet in swift, determined strides.

When he set her down next to the bed, but kept one arm around her waist, she didn't know how she felt about the realization he'd yet to speak to her.

Despite the fact Evan stood in front of him wearing nothing but her cutoff shorts and boots, she fought the red color she knew had spread across her face. Straightening her shoulders, she refused to be embarrassed. She'd asked the man for so much more than standing there half naked in front of him. Glancing up at him, she was surprised to see how dark his green eyes had turned. His jaw ticced as he stared at her bare chest.

"Ty—"

His gaze collided with hers. "My way, Evan. Got it?"

An unspoken battle of wills seemed to stretch between them. She lowered her gaze to his chest and gritted her teeth.

Before she could ask him why, Ty's fingers slid up her neck until he touched her jaw. She shivered at the contact, the first time he'd touched her intimately.

He applied pressure so she had to meet his gaze. Heated arousal reflected in his serious stare.

"Understand?"

His softer tone and the look of sheer desire in his gaze melted her stubborn resolve to remain on equal footing.

For now.

She started to nod, but his mouth covered hers, stopping her movement. His lips were warm, soft and so very persuasive. She opened her mouth and welcomed the slow, sensual glide of his tongue alongside hers.

Evan put her hands around his neck and started to step closer, but Ty cupped her breasts, his fingers gripping the full, soft tissue. Did he do that on purpose to keep her at a distance? When she tried to pull him closer, Ty slid his fingers to her nipples and rolled the tips between his thumb and index finger.

Pleasure radiated from her breasts and jolted straight down to her sex. Evan's heart raced as her fingers dug into the flesh on his shoulders.

Ty broke their kiss and let go of her. "Take off the rest of your clothes and lie down."

"What?" His commanding tone surprised her.

His steady gaze held hers. "You heard me."

Evan straightened her spine. "I don't take orders—"

"It wasn't an order. It was a request."

Evan bit her lower lip. Why was she fighting him? She'd said she wanted this.

When she met his inscrutable gaze, she realized why. She wanted Ty to be just as involved, just as caught up. She wanted to shake that impenetrable control he'd built around himself. No, she wanted to blast it away!

As seconds ticked by, she glanced down to see his hands balled into fists by his sides as well as the huge bulge in his pants. He wanted.

Now it was her job to make him want it more.

With a determined tilt of her chin, she locked her gaze with his as she kicked off her boots and unbuttoned her shorts. She shimmied out of her shorts and underwear with a purposeful jiggle of her breasts before pulling off her socks with a sexy grin.

Her confidence faltered when she realized Ty's expression hadn't changed at her naked state. Uncertainty settled once more as she pulled the covers back and lay down on the bed.

Ty's gaze flicked toward the top of the bed. "Lean your back against the headboard."

Intrigued by his plan, Evan's pulse raced as she scooted up to the top of the bed. She shivered when her back met the cool wood of the tall headboard.

Ty pushed the covers to the bottom of the bed. Evan's gaze skimmed over his broad back as he sat down on the edge of the mattress to pull his boots off. Instead of dropping his shoes, he set the boots beside the bed as if purposefully taking his time. Every move he made seemed precise and controlled. As exciting as his calculated actions made her feel, she wanted nothing more than to see what he'd be like if he was pushed too far.

Ty took a pillow and stuffed it behind her back, then turned on the bed and faced her. Her heart raced as he placed his hands on either side of her legs. "Bend your knees."

Bend her knees? That would expose her completely. No way. She wanted to be on equal footing with him. "Take off your clothes," she countered.

Her expression must've given him a clue as to her thoughts, because he shook his head and continued in an even tone. "If you want this, you must completely let go of your inhibitions."

"What I *want* requires you to be just as naked," she shot back.

Ty raised his eyebrow in a deliberate challenge. "My—"

"I know, I know." Evan sighed and bent her knees. When she started to place her feet flat on the bed against her body, Ty climbed on the bed and captured her heels.

Her stomach fluttered and her sex ached when he placed his knees on the outside of each of her thighs, then settled his rear on his calves before he lowered her feet to the bed on either side of his thighs.

Now her body truly surrounded his. If she thought the position he suggested before would expose her, this position allowed no privacy whatsoever.

Ty leaned forward and slid the rubber band out of her hair. His gaze remained fixed on her hair as he ran his fingers through the curls.

Once he'd tossed the rubber band to the floor, he leaned forward and covered her hands with his on the bed. Evan held back her gasp of excitement when he placed a kiss against her neck. While Ty leaned close, she took a deep breath. Leather, musk and a faint soap smell. If she ran her tongue along his skin, would he taste salty from the day's sweaty activities? She had to know.

Evan slid her tongue across his shoulder. She was surprised when she felt Ty shudder.

He pulled back, green eyes narrowed. "My way, Evan."

He was salty. In more ways than one, yet he was still sexy as hell. "But—"

His hands tightened around hers.

"Are you saying I can't touch you?" she asked, incredulous.

"Not yet."

She let out an exasperated huff. "I just don't get you. How are we supposed to—"

Ty's mouth covered hers, cutting off her words. As his tongue thrust deep, tangling with hers, Evan's mind turned to mush. She pressed her lips against his, countering his aggressive kiss with her own.

God, could the man kiss! The act of his lips slanting over hers, while his tongue invaded and enticed her active response, sent pinpoints of excitement scattering throughout her body. She dug her toes in the bed and wished he'd let her hands go so she could explore his gorgeous body with more than just her eyes.

Ty moved his mouth to her ear. "Keep your hands right here."

"If I move my hands?" she challenged.

His serious green gaze met hers as he trailed his fingers across her shoulders in a light caress. "I'll stop."

Evan set her lips in a firm line and fisted her hands on the bed.

Ty's lips quirked upward, as if he knew just how much of a battle it was for her to keep her hands still. His fingers trailed over her collarbone, then dropped lower until they cupped the edges of her breasts. Evan's stomach tensed when he spoke. "You said you know your own body, but do you really?"

The pads of his fingers skimmed her sensitive skin until they came close to her nipples.

Her breathing increased and she noted his raised eyebrow as if he expected her to respond to his question. The stitches in his other eyebrow made him appear even more dark and intense now.

"Yes."

He plucked at her nipples then pinched them. "Do you touch your breasts when you're pleasing yourself?"

She shrugged, while trying to fight the desire slamming through her. "Not really."

"That's a shame." He shook his head, then twirled her nipples before pinching the tips once more. "*Every* part of your body, if stimulated properly, can elicit a sexual response, Evan."

He had her on the nipple thing. Her sex reacted instantly to his stimulation, throbbing in deep, aching need. As far as she was concerned, there was only one other place on her body that responded to touch in a sexual sense.

He raised an eyebrow at her silence. "You don't believe me?"

She skimmed her gaze down his cut chest and six-pack abs to the bulge in his pants. "I know what part of my body responds to sexual stimulation."

Ty set his jaw at her honest comment. Now why had that angered him? When he moved his hands to her arms once more, she wanted to wail.

He rubbed his fingers along her muscles then skimmed the

pads down the skin along the inside of her arms. Evan literally shuddered at his touch. She had no idea that skin could be so sensitive.

Ty ran his hands back up her arms then pressed his palms against the sides of her breasts as he cupped his fingers around her sides. His hands began to move in slow, circular motions down her sides until he reached her waist.

Evan dug her short nails into her hands to keep from grabbing the man and pulling him against her. The sexy look in his eyes told her he knew what he was doing to her. Gripping her waist, he slowly ran his thumbs over her belly button.

Her lower belly moved in and out with her rapid panting, while her insides pitched and fluttered in tense anticipation.

When he slid his index fingers between the crease where her legs met her body, Evan thought she was going to climax from the built-up anticipation. Heat flooded her channel as she throbbed in unfulfilled sexual desire.

Ty glanced down at her sex and smiled. "You're wet."

"That means I'm ready."

He shook his head at her snappy comment. "Not yet."

"Touch me, Ty," she begged.

"I am." His fingers continued their descent down the side of her sex, yet he didn't touch her.

Her stomach had begun to knot. She clamped her legs against his arms and panted out, "I can't take this."

Ty's serious gaze snapped to hers as he pulled her legs apart. "Yes, you can. I want to show you just how explosive it can be, Evan, not the quick orgasms you're used to experiencing, but a long, satisfying one. You have to trust me."

"Right now I want to *kill* you," she bit out between clenched teeth.

He ignored her anger and focused his gaze on her once more.

She moaned and rocked her hips when his fingers finally touched her highly sensitive skin. But Ty didn't just briefly touch her. He rubbed the pink skin slowly between his fingers as if he were touching the softest of flower petals. Evan bit back her moan when his fingertips traced all along the edges in tantalizing, teasing touches.

Evan gritted her teeth and closed her eyes at the sweet torture. If he didn't touch her soon, she was going to be arrested for committing murder. She could see her dad's shocked expression now. *"You killed him for delaying your orgasm?"*

"Open your eyes," he said, his voice gruff and edgy.

Evan's eyes snapped open. When she saw the pulse at his throat beating at a hard pace, she managed a smile. Good, she wasn't the only one affected.

Ty's finger ran along the inside edge of her entrance once more before he circled all the way around.

Evan bucked and whimpered, shutting her eyes.

"Look at me," he commanded. Evan's gaze locked with his. She sobbed when he finally slid a finger slightly slowly inside her. Her hips moved forward, encouraging a deeper exploration.

"Damn, you're tight and sopping wet," he gritted out.

"I told—" She cut herself off and moaned in sheer pleasure when he added another finger.

Ty began to move his fingers in and out of her body. When she moaned, he said, "You know I'm bigger than this, Evan...a lot bigger."

She heard the warning in his tone and rocked her hips in earnest, seeking relief. "I'm looking forward to it."

His gaze lowered to his hand between them. He seemed enthralled by the sight.

Evan panted as she lifted her hips to meet each of his thrusts. She was so close.

Ty's movements slowed and he withdrew his fingers to run them along the sensitive skin around her entrance once more. Her heart thumped so hard she could hear it in her own throat.

"Wh-why did you stop?" She gripped the sheet tight when he circled his finger around her clitoris.

Ty's steady gaze met hers as he slid his fingers inside her once more. Evan jerked her hips against him and relished the sensation of his fingers turning inside her, touching her thoroughly, intimately and very purposefully. He was methodical, leaving no section of her channel untouched before pressing on a wonderful spot deep inside.

Evan felt her orgasm approaching. She closed her eyes and tensed her body, ready to welcome the passionate tremors.

Ty started to withdraw his hand once more. Her eyes jerked open and she grabbed his wrist, holding him close to her. "No!"

His gaze darkened and his expression turned hard. His fingers stilled inside her. "Do you want this? Want to come so bad you can't stand it?"

When she bit her lip and nodded, he skimmed his fingers across her hot-spot once more in a tender caress. "Then trust me."

She released his hand and let out an unsteady, sexually frustrated breath.

TY WATCHED the myriad expressions filter across Evan's face —frustration, fear, anger then reluctant acceptance.

Curls of strawberry-blonde hair stuck to the side of her face. Her cheeks were flushed and her skin literally glowed from her exertions. He'd always thought redheads were hot, but he came to the conclusion that a touch of red in blonde hair made him ache. Evan was so damn sexy, so sincere and natural in her responses...he'd never wanted a woman more than he did this one. She held nothing back. He saw each glimmer of emotion scatter across her face as she experienced them. It was the most erotic, satisfying sex he'd ever had with a woman, and he'd yet to slide inside her.

She began to whimper and roll her hips as he brushed her G-spot over and over again. Primal male satisfaction roared within him. He wanted to beat his chest—damn, he wanted to fuck her so bad he was sure he'd have blue balls before this session was over.

But he was determined to make this an experience Evan would never forget. To show her how satisfying sex with a person who took his time with her could be, especially if she delayed her release until she couldn't hold back any longer.

At the same time he rubbed her hot-spot deep inside, Ty pressed his palm flat on her lower belly, making every stroke against her G-spot that much more tactile. Then he moved his thumb over her clit and rolled the tiny bud in small circles.

"Ohmigod, Ty...I can't."

She began to buck hard against him.

"Look at me."

Evan opened her eyes and the arousal he saw there almost did him in. Clenching his jaw, he reined in his raging lust. If he didn't, Evan wouldn't know what hit her. He'd be inside her before her orgasm stopped.

She'd risen up on her hands to press her body down hard against the heel of his hand. As her channel began to contract around his fingers and her arms began to shake, Ty couldn't resist any longer. While he continued to stroke inside her body, he cupped the back of her neck and yanked her close.

When his mouth covered hers, Evan wrapped her arms around his shoulders. As she rode the last remnants of her climax, she tugged on his hair, moaned against his mouth and pressed closer. If that didn't tell him just how much she enjoyed what he was doing to her, nothing would.

The momentum of her actions threw them both back against the bed. Ty was so caught up, he reacted purely on animal instinct.

Withdrawing his hand from her body, he quickly rolled her underneath him. His fingers speared through her hair at the same time he thrust his tongue deep in her mouth. Without conscious thought he pressed his aching cock against her wet heat and ground against her. He relished the sensation of her naked breasts crushed against his chest, while the smell of her sex further seduced him with its alluring aroma.

Evan panted at his actions and dug her fingernails into his back. She wrapped her legs tight around his hips and locked him to her.

Ty rocked against her sweet body as if his hips had a mind all their own. His jeans did little to buffer the erotic sensations his actions elicited. When he felt his orgasm approaching and realized his mind wasn't going to be able to slow it down, he jerked his mouth from hers. No! It wasn't supposed to happen like this. He was determined to remain detached, in total control.

He ignored the confused look on Evan's face as he got up from the bed.

"Ty?"

She sat up on her elbows. Her breasts were begging to be touched, her hair was a gorgeous mess, her lips were swollen from his hard kisses. He wanted nothing more than to sink into her body again and again. The thought of being the very first man to do so slammed through his mind, front and center. But not like this. Not when he didn't have a handle on his desires.

"My way," was all he managed to grunt out before he grabbed his boots and walked out of the bedroom, heading for the front door.

8

E van stood in her quiet house and shoved clothes across the wooden rod in her bedroom closet with a disgruntled sigh. Nothing. Not one damn stylish piece of clothing in the whole lot.

"What does that say about you?" she mumbled aloud as she blew an errant curl out of her face.

She glanced at her watch and her stomach tensed when she realized she had less than two hours to transform herself into a sleek, sophisticated woman before Harm and Jena's party started. Harm's parents were very active in the community, so she knew everyone who was anyone would be there... including Doctor Lily Shelton. It irked her that she felt this strong desire to outshine Lily.

She pulled a blue dress she'd forgotten about out of the closet. Laying the soft fabric against her chest, she turned and faced herself in the mirror.

She scanned the freckles on her nose then moved her gaze to her broad shoulders and mammoth height, and came to the annoying conclusion she couldn't compete with Lily's sleek, classy look and petite stature.

Throwing the dress on her bed, she frowned at herself in the mirror. Why was it so important that she grab Ty's attention tonight? Her cheeks turned red at the memory of what they shared earlier. The passion and intensity between them blew her away. Ty did what he set out to do. He showed her that a man with the right sexual knowledge could make her body quake with a mind-blowing orgasm.

But what swept her heart away wasn't only the soul-jarring climax she'd experienced, but Ty's lips on hers, the sensation of him rolling her underneath him and pressing against her as if he couldn't stop himself. In that moment, she realized that more than losing her virginity, what she wanted from Ty was fierce, unbridled, out-of-control desire—for her. Something she had a depressing feeling he'd once felt and, based on his reaction today, probably still felt for Lily.

With one last determined glance in the mirror, she squared her shoulders and turned back to the closet to find a pair of shoes.

TY KEPT one eye on the hotel's ballroom doorway while he half listened to his mom talking to Harm's parents.

"Having a good time, Ty?" His uncle Rick clapped him on the shoulder.

Ty turned to his uncle. "Hey, Uncle Rick. I'm glad you made it. Have you spoken to Jena yet?"

Rick gave him a broad smile. The effect spread his black mustache across his open face. "Yep, met her fiancé, too. She seems very happy." His smile lowered and a sad look crossed his face. "I wish my brother had lived to see his little girl getting married."

Ty put his hand on his uncle's thick shoulder. "I think my dad would be very glad to know his brother came all the way to Texas to see his niece get married."

His uncle's smile returned. "I know you're giving Jena away, but I told her I'd like to stand up and give her a kiss and a hug for her dad before she takes her vows."

Ty nodded and smiled. "I'm sure she'd love that."

Turning to Harm's parents, whom Jena had introduced him to earlier, Ty said, "Mr. and Mrs. Steele, I'd like you to meet our uncle, Rick Hudson."

While Rick spoke to Harm's parents, Ty pushed his suit jacket sleeve back and glanced at his watch. Where was Evan? The party had started half an hour ago. Guilt tightened his chest. He'd left her rather abruptly. When he'd come back to the house, she was gone. He hoped the reason she hadn't shown yet wasn't because she was upset at the way he'd left. But damn it, the woman had affected him more than he wanted or expected her to.

Familiar floral perfume with seductive jasmine notes surrounded him before a small, feminine hand encircled the crook of his arm.

"Hello, Ty."

His gaze locked with Lily's dark brown eyes and his stomach tensed. "Hey, Lily."

She kept her hand on his arm and her gaze drifted across his face. "You left before I could tell you to keep your wound clean, and if you're still in town after two weeks, to come back to have the stitches removed."

Ty didn't respond. He scanned the crowd sitting down and eating, then his gaze moved past the people on the dance floor to the room's entrance.

"You're so quiet. Not at all like the Ty I knew."

Ty heard the knowing smile in her tone. He didn't bother looking down at her when he responded. "I'm not the same person I was back then."

"I'm sure you aren't. You're a man now." She tugged on his arm. "You seem so tense. Come dance with me for old times' sake."

Ty allowed her to pull him out on the dance floor. He felt like a piece of hard metal bent to its limit; a tightly wound spring, ready to snap, but the sensation of her hand on his arm told him he needed to find out for sure if he'd finally gotten over her. How would it feel to hold her in his arms again after all these years?

As he put his arm around Lily's lower back and held her other hand to lead, he noted just how small and fragile she was. Even wearing three-inch heels, she just reached his chin. Tonight she'd worn her straight black hair down. The soft strands landed just over her shoulders. Her black spaghetti-strapped dress scooped low to reveal her ample cleavage—cleavage he'd very much appreciated as a randy teenager.

"This suit looks custom-made." Lily's gaze followed her hand as she ran it across his shoulder and the expensive black fabric. A pleased smile crossed her features as she met his gaze. "So you're an architect who owns his own business. You've done very well for yourself."

He raised an eyebrow. "You've been checking up on me?"

She laughed. "How else was I supposed to find out? It's not like you were forthcoming."

Ty shrugged. "It wasn't relevant."

"True. But I was curious. Didn't you ever wonder about me? Weren't you ever curious to know how I turned out?"

His entire body tensed. How many times had he wondered what had happened to Lily? What type of man it took to make her happy? "Not really."

A hurt expression crossed her face. "You asked me to marry you once, Ty. Are you saying I meant so little to you?"

Ty's jaw tightened. "That was a long time ago."

Her lips thinned as if she were irritated by his abrupt tone before a smile settled on her lips. "Yes, it was a long time ago. We were both very young, but one thing has stayed with me all these years."

"What was that?"

Lily slid her arm up his shoulder and cupped the back of his neck. Pressing her chest against his, she pulled on his neck until he moved close enough for her to whisper in his ear.

"You're the best lover I ever had."

Shock ricocheted through Ty at her revelation. All the time he'd spent thinking he didn't measure up. Years of sexual self-doubt in his early twenties, wondering if his performance in the sack was the reason he couldn't convince Lily to marry him, wasted. The heavy weight slid off his shoulders as if he'd just shed an Alaskan winter coat.

At the same time he straightened to look Lily in the face, he caught sight of Evan standing ten feet away, staring at them.

Evan started to walk away, but Chad grasped her elbow. The jerk-off whispered something in her ear before he clasped her hand and tugged her out onto the dance floor.

Lily's soft fingers turned Ty's jaw until his gaze met hers.

"Did you hear what I said?" Her dark gaze searched his as she wrapped her arms around his neck.

Ty stopped dancing and pulled her arms down from his neck. "Like you said...we were just kids."

Lily gave him a siren's smile. Her seductive gaze swept over him, assessing and appreciating every inch. "Oh, I know that. If you were good back then with *no* sexual experience, I can only imagine what you're like now."

Her compliment landed on him like a load of wet cement, heavy and sticky but quickly turning hard and stiff. He couldn't believe he'd thought she'd dumped him because he was a lousy lay.

As anger swept through him, Ty's gaze drifted back to Chad's arms around Evan's waist. The bastard had started massaging her lower back. Her wavy hair just brushed her exposed back where the navy dress plunged all the way to the base of her spine.

When Ty looked at Evan, his pulse raced and he instantly hardened. It didn't matter what she wore. Then again, he liked her best wearing nothing at all. The better to enjoy her long, shapely legs and sweet, honeyed skin.

"Ty."

He had to drag his attention from Evan and Chad. As he narrowed his gaze on the woman pouting before him, Ty realized two certainties—just how much he wanted Evan and just how fucking over Lily he was. She didn't hold a candle to the way Evan made him feel. With Evan, he *burned* with the need to touch her.

"You got what you wanted in life, no one to hold you back from your professional goals, Doctor Shelton. I hope you're happy with it."

Ty walked off the dance floor and headed straight for the bar. "Shot of whisky, straight up."

The bartender nodded and poured him a drink.

Ty watched Chad lean close and brush his lips down Evan's neck. He picked up the shot glass and downed the drink in one swig. Fury, unlike anything he'd ever experienced in his life swept through him, burning just like the alcohol did going down. Everything he'd learned, breathing techniques, focus, emotional control—gone. All because a man dared to touch the woman he wanted.

Wanted.

Hell yeah, he wanted Evan. Wanted to feel her sexy legs wrapped around his hips, wanted to hear her moaning as he slid inside her, then screaming when he began to thrust deep. He wanted her to come over and over...all because of him.

Only for him.

Gritting his teeth, he was glad his jacket covered the raging hard-on that pushed against the fly of his pants.

Lily chose that moment to walk up and order a glass of white wine. Her gaze followed his line of sight. After the bartender poured her glass, she picked it up and took a sip.

She turned to walk away, but paused just a moment to glance at him over her shoulder. "Since I doubt you'll be coming by my office to have your stitches removed, why don't you ask Doctor Masters to take care of removing them for you."

Ty frowned at the sarcasm in Lily's voice. Was she jealous that he was interested in someone who didn't hold a professional job? Evan seemed very dedicated to her career, regardless if she didn't have initials by her last name. He'd used that as an excuse to give Lily a hard time, but Ty didn't give a shit about the professional part. It all boiled down to the fact he was a selfish bastard. He wasn't interested in a woman who sent him to the backseat for her career.

Jena's voice drew his attention. "You've put in an appearance, big brother. You can leave any time you'd like."

Ty slid his gaze her way. "What makes you think I want to leave?"

She gave him a sisterly smile. "Oh, I dunno. Maybe because you haven't taken your eyes off Evan since she walked in the room."

Ty looked down at the shot glass he rolled in his palm. "You afraid I'm going to make another scene?"

"Are you?"

When he snapped his gaze to hers, mischief danced in her vivid blue eyes.

The slow song was coming to the end. A devilish smile tugged at Ty's lips as he set the shot glass on the counter. "Not as long as I can pry Evan out of the cocky bastard's tight clutches."

"Allow me." Before Ty could say a word, his sister started across the dance floor toward the couple.

"Chad, I'm so glad to see you could make it." Jena walked up with her hand outstretched and a broad smile on her face.

Chad shifted his gaze to Jena and put his hand out to shake hers. "Hey, Jena, or should I say, Soon-to-be Mrs. Harmon Steele. Thanks for the invitation."

Jena tugged on Chad's hand. "Your dad wanted me to introduce you to my family. My Uncle Rick's an attorney. I told him you'd just passed the bar. Why don't you come and meet him."

Chad's grip on Evan's waist started to slip as he allowed Jena to tug him toward her. Evan knew Chad planned to follow in his father's political footsteps. He was also the kind of guy who never passed up an opportunity to make another contact. In that respect, he was definitely his father's son.

"You finally made it." The sound of Ty's deep voice made Evan's heart skip several beats.

Chad's grip on her waist instantly tightened when he heard Ty behind them. He turned and narrowed his gaze on Jena's brother. "Evan's here with me."

Evan stepped out of Chad's hold, fed up with both men. "I'm not 'here' with anyone." Nodding toward Jena, she smiled. "I take it the rehearsal went well?"

Jena laughed as she tucked her hand around Chad's arm. "Of course, but despite a great rehearsal, I know one should never expect everything to go perfectly on one's wedding day."

Evan smiled her understanding then looked up at Chad. "Go with Jena."

His blue gaze darted between Evan and Ty, then narrowed. "I'll go if you promise me a dance tomorrow after the wedding."

She felt the weight of Ty's heavy gaze on her, but she refused to look his way. "Okay, I'll dance with yo—"

Chad pulled her close and kissed her hard, cutting off her words. Evan didn't even have time to react. Chad broke their kiss and cast a triumphant smirk Ty's way before he walked off with Jena.

Evan's stomach tightened at Ty's nearness, but anger still welled within her. She'd seen the way Lily had wrapped herself around him. Ty didn't seem to mind one bit. As a matter of fact, he seemed to have a tight grip on the woman's perfectly pinched, no-wider-than-the-span-of-a-man's-hand waist. *Grrrr!*

"Evan."

She ignored him as she headed for the entryway. She'd come to the party as she promised Jena she would, but she refused to hang with Ty. It wasn't like they had any type of commitment or anything, but for God's sake the man had had his hand inside her, stroking her to climax just a few hours ago. Her heels clicked on the hard floor outside the ballroom with each determined step she took down the hall toward the hotel's entrance.

"Evan."

Despite her frustration with Ty, her stomach fluttered at the sound of his voice so close behind her. "It's okay, Ty. I've decided to let you off the hook from our agreement."

Evan gasped when Ty grabbed her arm and opened a door that led to an empty ballroom. Yanking her inside, he closed the door and faced her. The dim lighting in the room allowed her to see the anger reflected in his expression as he jerked his head back toward the way they had come.

"Why? Because you'd rather have that prick's cock in you instead?"

The sound of Evan's hand connecting with Ty's face resounded in the large empty room. "That was out of line!"

Ty grabbed her wrist before she could pull away. His green gaze glittered with anger and something else as he used his hold to yank her toward him.

When his mouth landed on hers, hard and demanding, Evan let out a surprised yelp, which came out sounding like a muffled *hmmmph*. Ty's lips didn't just claim hers. He possessed her with his aggressive kiss. His tongue thrust deep and his hands moved to her back before they slid down her spine to cup her rear through her dress. It was the kind of kiss that had nothing to do with control and everything to do with raw, staking-his-claim desire.

As excited as Ty's kiss made her feel, she wasn't about to let the man call her out about Chad without giving as good as she got. Pushing against his chest, she broke their heated kiss. "Don't you think Lily will wonder where you went?"

He gave her a puzzled look. "What are you talking about?"

She shrugged and tried to pull out of his arms, but Ty just tightened his hold.

"Answer me, damn it."

"Jena told me you and Lily dated a long time ago. I guess when you saw her all dressed up, you decided to pick up where you left off."

Ty's gaze dropped to her lips and he backed her up against the door. "There's only one woman I want."

With her back flat against the solid surface, Ty pressed his chest against her breasts and finished in a husky tone, "You're the only woman I'm so hot to get inside of I can't think about anything else." He pressed his lips to her neck and lifted her off the floor so he could rock his erection against her mound. "I can't wait to slide inside your sweet, tight body, Eve."

His words went straight to her toes and her pulse thrummed in excitement. Evan cupped the back of his neck as his lips covered hers once more. When he set her down and his hands began to lift the hem of her dress higher, her heart hammered and her belly tensed in pent-up sexual frustration. Of their own accord, her hands moved to unbutton his jacket, then she slid her hands down his tight stomach to unbutton and unzip his pants. She didn't give a damn if her first time was against a door. So long as it was with Ty and just like this —as passionate as it could be.

His warm hands connected with the back of her bare legs, sending shivers down her spine. Evan moaned against his mouth. Her sounds must've spurred him on because he gripped her thighs and lifted her. Before she could utter a word, he rammed his cloth-covered cock against her. Her underwear and his boxer briefs prevented what they both seemed to desperately want, yet the barrier of clothes between them somehow turned her on even more.

As he began to rock against her, she wrapped her arms and legs tight around him, pausing to say between heated kisses, "I think we're a bit overdressed."

"Shhhh," he said, then moved his lips near her ear. His thrusts grew stronger as he rode her against the door. "You're so damn wet. God, I'm so aroused by your heat I can't think straight." His grip tightened on her buttocks and his shoulders tensed underneath her arms as he ground himself against her. She cried out at the erotic sensations building inside her.

Ty exhaled in a pained hiss as if he were trying his best not to lose it. He lowered her to the ground, and she felt his knuckles rubbing her sex as he shoved his cock through the opening in his boxers.

Evan's heart pounded even faster when Ty slid his fingers down her mound to cup her in a possessive hold. The sensation of his fingers skimming across her sex outside her wet underwear only made her heart beat harder. She gripped his shoulders and felt them suddenly tense underneath her fingers.

"Wait. I've got a condom."

She shook her head. "No, don't stop. I'm on the Pill."

A surprised expression crossed his face. "A virgin on the Pill?"

She half-laughed. "It keeps me regular."

Nodding, he rasped, "I'm glad I don't have to stop." His intense gaze locked with hers at the same time he jerked her underwear to the side. Her heart pounded in excited, stuttering jolts at his aggressive action, then revved right back up when he slid his erection down her mons toward her entrance. God, she was ready!

"Has anyone seen Evan?" a man called down the hall, his voice frantic as he ran past.

Evan froze, her heart pounding out of control. Pushing on Ty's chest, she said, "I'm sorry. I have to go."

Ty held her tight for a couple of seconds as if he wasn't going to let her go. When he finally released her, Evan straightened her underwear and lowered her dress, then she opened the door and closed it behind her.

"Dave, over here," he heard her call out.

Ty quickly fixed his pants and buttoned his jacket then exited the room. When he closed the door behind him, an older man in a bloodstained T-shirt was standing a few feet away talking to Evan in rapid bursts.

"She's bleeding everywhere. That nasty dog attacked her. Please, Evan, you've got to save our little Brandi."

"Calm down, Dave." Evan put a hand on the man's arm.

The gray-haired man took a couple of gulps of air, then nodded. "I'm calm."

She pulled her hand away and gave a reassuring smile. "Okay, good. Where is Brandi now?"

The old man's hand shook as he pointed toward the

entrance to the hotel lobby. "She's wrapped in a towel in the car. My wife's holding her."

Evan patted his shoulder. "Okay. Bring her straight to my office. I'll meet you there in just a few minutes."

Her office? "Is the vet back in town then?" Ty asked.

The old man gave him a confused look. "Huh?" He pointed to Evan. "She *is* the vet," he said before he took off in a hurried pace toward the lobby.

Ty met Evan's gaze and saw the truth in her eyes. "You're the town vet?"

Evan gave him a half-smile. "Guilty." A moment of silence stretched between them. Ty was so surprised, he didn't know what to say. The comment Lily made earlier now made perfect sense. She must've assumed he knew Evan was a vet and was digging at him for choosing Evan over her. Suddenly, his mind flipped back to the black bag Evan had brought to tend Daisy's wound. The initials on the bag had read EJM, DVM. Why hadn't they registered in his mind until now?

Evan cleared her throat and pushed a lock of hair behind her ear. "I'd better go meet Dave. It sounds like Brandi's pretty torn up."

As shocked as he was by this latest discovery about Evan's career, Ty wasn't ready to let her go. "Is there anything I can do to help? Bring you some clothes?"

"I always keep a change of clothes in my car." She smiled and started to turn away, calling over her shoulder, "I'll see you later, okay?"

"Sure."

While Evan rushed toward the entrance of the hotel, Ty's gaze locked on her sweet ass swaying to the click of her heels. His groin tightened all over again when she cast her gaze back at him one last time before she walked outside. Once Evan was out of sight, the realization he'd almost lost complete control with her against the door in the ballroom sank in full force. Damn, she'd had him so caught up. Ty locked his jaw, both annoyed and relieved at the interruption.

Why had she lied to him about her profession? He steeled himself, his shoulders tensing in sheer determination. He would find out the answer...and he would damn well hold his emotions in check when they had sex. This time around, he was going into it with his eyes wide open. No expectations, no strings attached, period. Evan would get what she wanted and so would he—a roll in the hay with a gorgeous woman, who was turning out to be full of intriguing layers he never would've imagined.

Evan entered Double D's house as quietly as she could. It was almost eleven. The emergency surgery had taken a lot longer than she'd anticipated, but she'd managed to save the mangled dog. Brandi would look like a refugee for a while, but Evan hoped the small pooch thought twice before tangling with a dog seven times her size again.

Ty was asleep on the couch. Even with the air-conditioning cranked up, he slept with no shirt and a thin sheet covering his lower body. She walked up to stare at his gorgeous chest for a few seconds.

The memory of their encounter in the empty ballroom would be burned in her head for a long time to come—the intensity and sheer spontaneity had blown her away. And still...he seemed to hold back a little. A smile tilted the corners of her lips. At least she got to see and feel some of his steely control slip down a notch or two.

Evan let out a quiet sigh and headed for her bedroom and a much-needed shower.

After she'd pulled off her clothes, she stepped under the pounding spray. The hot water pelted her skin like warm, soothing fingers massaging her tired muscles.

She wished she could read Ty's mind when he found out she was the town vet. He definitely looked surprised, but he hadn't appeared put off by it. If anything, he'd appeared intrigued. At least he seemed to accept her vet status.

She started to pick up her soap but her gaze strayed to Ty's bar of soap sitting next to hers in the dish attached to the wall.

Evan couldn't resist picking up the brown-hued bar and inhaling. It smelled of sandalwood and other spices she couldn't identify. She ran his soap over her skin and reveled in Ty's scent floating in the air around her. She lifted her forearm, put her nose to her freshly washed skin and inhaled deeply. Her stomach tensed and her heart jerked at the appealing scent. She'd have to ask him what brand the soap was so she could buy some. Then she could keep a bit of Ty with her long after he left.

The thought of Ty leaving made her chest constrict as she shampooed her hair and rinsed the suds out. *Get a grip, girl. You haven't even had sex with the man yet.* But it wasn't just about the sex with Ty. He was intelligent and seductively intense. He stuck to his convictions and stepped in without a moment's hesitation for those who needed help. He was exactly the type of man she wanted to marry one day.

Too bad he lived fifteen hundred miles away. She shut the shower off with a determined twist of her wrist. At least she had him for a couple more days. The sight of the water draining out of the shower, steam floating in the air and Ty's scent lingering in the room conjured the memory of Ty stroking his erection during his shower.

He'd seemed so in command of himself and his physical responses. The sheer restraint was a turn-on unlike any she'd ever seen. Her vivid thoughts made her sex throb in excited awareness. Shrugging off the seductive sensations gripping her on both a mental and physical level, Evan grabbed the towel off the shower rod and wrapped it around herself.

Once she'd towel-dried her hair, she tucked the towel's end between her breasts and pulled the shower curtain back. Evan let out a small gasp, her heart racing at the sight of Ty standing in the doorway in his black boxer briefs. He leaned against the doorjamb, not at all embarrassed by his obvious erection pushing the cotton material outward.

He didn't say a word as he walked toward her. Evan's pulse leapt at the rugged look of his tousled dark hair and five o'clock shadow. He stepped right into her personal space, his green gaze studying her with a palpable heat that made her breath catch. When he reached for the towel's end tucked between her breasts, her stomach flip-flopped then did a triple somersault. As he grasped the fabric, his knuckles nudged her cleavage. The erotic sensation made her knees threaten to give way.

Ty's gaze dropped to her body as he peeled the towel away. He scanned every inch in a slow, leisurely sweep.

Chill bumps formed on her skin while she waited to see his eyes again. What would she see reflected in their depths?

But Ty didn't return his gaze to hers. Instead, he surprised her when he dropped the towel on the floor and swiftly picked her up, carrying her out of the bathroom.

Evan's pulse raced as her arms settled around his broad shoulders. Defined muscles flexed underneath her hands. She ran her palms across his warm skin and inhaled. Ty's scent reached out and grabbed her at a deep, gut-wrenching level. She pressed her nose against his neck and took another deep breath. Evan realized that no soap could ever capture Ty's true essence. His own masculine smell mingled with the soap's aroma to create a scent that totally seduced her.

Ty laid her down on the bed and then straightened to step out of his boxers. When his underwear hit the floor, her gaze locked on his hard erection and her body clenched in response. The man was definitely well-endowed. Every muscle inside her stilled when he placed his knee on the bed.

His hands hit the mattress on either side of her head as he leaned over her. While the light from the bathroom cast his face in dark shadows, she knew her face was fully exposed. She didn't care. Let him see the desire in her gaze. Maybe it would help him open up a little. Evan placed her hands on his shoulders as he moved closer.

Ty's lips brushed against hers in a feather-light kiss. Her fingers flexed on his shoulders as she pressed her mouth against his, ready for more. When she ran her tongue along his lower lip, a low growl rumbled against her mouth before Ty pulled away to lay down behind her.

He cupped her breast and used his hold to pull her back flush against his hard chest, aligning his muscular body with hers. Evan sighed in excited anticipation.

Her heart melted when she felt him rub his nose in her

hair and heard him inhale her scent. Then it skipped several beats as she waited.

And waited.

A few seconds later, her anticipation turned to confusion. She felt Ty's erection against her backside. His fingers were sure to leave imprints on her breast, he held her in such a firm grip, yet the man remained perfectly still.

Reaching back, she slid her fingers up his neck, spearing them through his thick, silky hair. "Ty?"

"Shhh," he whispered against her neck, sending shivers skidding down her spine. Releasing her breast, he pulled the covers over them, then clasped her hip under the covers in a possessive hold.

Still he didn't move.

She wanted him so much, her belly began to cramp. Evan closed her eyes for several seconds, seeking patience. She failed miserably.

"Are we sleeping?" She tried to keep the frustration out of her voice.

Ty pressed his erection against her buttocks as he flattened his palm across her belly. "Yeah, we are. You've had a long day and night. You need to rest."

I need you sliding inside me, she wanted to scream.

She turned over onto her back. "Is this another 'my way' thing?"

He chuckled and kissed her on the forehead. "I guess it is."

Hooking her leg across his thigh, Evan shoved Ty onto his back. "Hell no!" she said as she straddled his hips and rested her sex against his erection. "Tonight we're doing things *my* way."

9

Ty's chest tensed underneath her palms as his hands surrounded her hips. "I know you're exhausted, Evan. We can wait until tomorrow."

Determination washed over her and she began to rock her hips, rubbing her hot moisture along the length of his cock.

The veins in Ty's neck surfaced and his fingers tightened on her hips, slowing her movements. "Evan," he warned. Now that their positions were switched, the light behind her revealed the heated desire burning in his gaze and the look of tension on his face. The man wanted her and was mentally fighting himself. The realization made her want him that much more.

Evan leaned forward and touched her nipples to his chest as she whispered against his ear, "Tonight, no more holding back." At the same time she lowered her entrance against the tip of his cock.

When her soft heat came in contact with his body, Ty's

hips jerked. His action caused his erection to barely slide inside her. It was a surprising, seductive tease.

Evan bit back her moan. She planted a kiss on his neck and lowered her body fully against his, blanketing him with her skin. "I want to feel your body against mine when you slide inside me. I've waited long enough."

Demanding hands gripped her hips and his lips grazed her neck. "Then it'll be my way," he ground out as his hips began to rock.

Evan felt his thickness moving deeper inside her, his actions slow, measured, precise. She moaned at the wonderful sensation, but she also realized he was doing it again—taking control while keeping himself in a kind of buffered state. It was as if he wanted their physical joining, without losing control of himself in the process.

"I told you we're doing it my way." Before Ty could stop her, she put her hands on his shoulders and shoved his hard shaft deep inside her channel, joining their bodies.

Her swift movement forced Ty to fill and stretch her completely. Piercing pain shot though her walls, making her eyes water. She gulped back her scream and buried her head against his shoulder.

"Damn it, Evan!" Ty's hands slid from her hips to cup her buttocks, his touch tender...protective.

She heard the anger and censure in his tone, but Evan didn't care. She wanted him to let go, to totally give in to his desires—all of them.

Neither one of them moved for a few seconds.

Finally Ty kissed her temple. "Are you okay?"

The pain had subsided to a dull ache. Evan nodded her head, then pushed herself to a seated position.

Her aggressive change of position caused his cock to shove deep inside her. She winced at the sharp pain.

Ty slid his hands to her upper back. "Give yourself more of an angle, sweetheart," he said in a husky tone at the same time he pulled her forward.

Evan bent her elbows a little and did as he suggested. Sheer pleasure quickly replaced the ache. She closed her eyes and moaned, savoring the decadent sensation of Ty's hard heat buried so deep, filling her wall to wall.

Though he'd moved his hands back to her hips, Ty hadn't said a word. Evan opened her eyes as she began to rock her hips.

Ty's eyes were closed and the tendons on his neck stood out as his hold on her hips tightened. She could tell he was concentrating.

"Look at me," she whispered. She had to see the desire in his eyes, to know he felt something more than what his body was telling her.

Ty's green gaze locked with hers and the tortured look almost took her breath away. It was as if he wanted so badly to let go, but he couldn't allow himself the luxury.

"You may be leaving day after tomorrow, but I'm determined you'll be flying out of Texas well spent, Ty Hudson. You feel too damn good and I plan to keep you in bed as long as I can."

The color of his eyes shifted to a green so dark, his eyes looked black. He flashed a sexy grin and began to thrust upward with each of her downward movements.

Evan arched her back at his aggressive and very effective movements. She felt stretched and full and very fulfilled. Her breasts tingled and her heart raced while her entire body flushed with renewed heat.

When Ty feathered his fingers across her nipples, her entire belly clenched in excited anticipation. "Touch me," she whispered.

Ty's gaze held hers as he rolled her nipples between his fingers. Evan's rocking pace increased and her breathing came out in short, erratic pants. Exquisite pleasure shot through her body.

She closed her eyes.

"Open your eyes. I want to watch you come."

Her eyes flew open at his comment.

"You were right. You're helluva lot tighter than your mouth," he said in a strained tone.

"And you're a helluva lot bigger than my fingers," she panted back with a half-laugh.

When she finished speaking, Ty thrust hard and deep at the same time he pinched her nipples. "The better to make you scream."

The deep timbre of his voice skidded down her spine, while all the sensations slamming into her at once caused tremors of pleasure to scatter throughout her body. Delicious sexual arousal built to its highest pitch within her.

Wave after wave of sheer ecstasy started in her channel and splintered all the way down to her fingers and her toes in heated, tingling bursts as her orgasm took over.

Ty moved his hands to her hips and used his grip to bury himself even deeper while she gyrated her hips, wanting her orgasm to last forever. "That's it, sweetheart. Take all of me."

AND EVAN DID. She pushed down, pressing her body hard against Ty's, taking him into her as deep as she could. She rode her explosive climax until the wonderful tremors stopped and her body shook all over in the aftermath.

Sweat glistened on Ty's chest. He was still hard and impaled so far inside her that she felt his heartbeat at the base of his cock. The rapid thump told her what he refused to...just how much he wanted to let go.

She leaned forward and planted a kiss on his hard chest, then flicked her tongue around his nipple until the tiny nub raised up enough for her to nip at it with her teeth.

Ty moaned and his hips jerked at her stimulation. One hand threaded through her hair, cupping the back of her head while the other caressed her rear.

Evan turned her head and laid it next to Ty's chest for a brief second. Ty's heart pounded against her cheek. She smiled at the telltale sign, then pushed herself back to a seated position.

Her gaze locked with his. "Ready to go for a ride, Yank?"

Ty cocked his eyebrow at her comment. Before he could respond she pulled herself completely off him, then slammed back down, burying him to the hilt.

"Shit, Evan!" he ground out as his hips moved of their own accord. He gave as good as he got, but Evan refused to climax without him this time.

"This ride doesn't stop until you're over the edge."

Ty groaned. "Is that a challenge?"

"No, it's a promise." Evan gave him a siren's smile as she reached behind her and cupped his sac in a firm grip.

Ty grunted and a surprised expression filtered across his face. "Easy," he warned with a half-groan, half-chuckle.

"I know a bit or two about male physiology." Her smile widened and she ran two fingers past his sac to press on the sensitive skin underneath them.

Ty let out a low growl. Before she knew what hit her, Ty had her back flat against the bed. He'd moved so fast, he took her breath away.

His hands speared through her hair and his mouth slanted across her lips at the same time his body covered hers.

Evan moaned and accepted his first deep thrust with relish. She put her feet flat on the bed and raised her hips, ready for him to withdraw and piston into her again and again. This was exactly what she wanted...Ty letting go.

Ty pulled out and rammed into her once more. His stubble scraped the soft skin around her mouth as his tongue tangled with hers. His kiss was hungry, dark, possessive and so utterly seductive that for a few seconds she just lay there kissing him while their bodies remained locked together, throbbing, waiting for them to move.

"Think you can handle me?" His rampant breathing was hot against her neck.

Evan ran her hands across his muscular back and down his spine until she cupped his hard buttocks. "If you're not thrusting hard enough, I'm gonna tell ya, darlin'."

Ty let out a strained chuckle then planted a kiss on her neck. "Don't worry. I want you so bad, I just thought you should have fair warning."

Evan bit back her moan of pleasure when he began to move his hips, each thrust harder and deeper than the last. His pace was rough and hard and, damn, it felt so good.

Evan relished the sensation of his muscular chest pressing her to the bed as his body moved inside her. The entire experience felt erotic, heated and so very right with Ty. His body ground against hers, driving her insane with intense pleasure. She began to pant as her heart hammered out of control.

"Bend your knees and wrap them around me."

Evan wasn't sure where he was going with his command, but she wrapped her legs around his hips.

Ty's breathing came out in harsh gusts. "Hold your legs as high as you can."

She didn't really want to change her position. It felt pretty damn good just the way she was.

Ty kissed her jaw then the soft spot behind her ear. "The angle will send you through the roof."

"When you put it that way..." She grabbed her shins and pulled them higher up his back. At the same time Ty came down with a forceful thrust.

Evan let out a keening moan as her body instantly began to spasm around him once more. This time her orgasm seemed to go bone-deep. Evan's heart thrummed at a jackrabbit's pace as her body contracted around Ty's erection again and again.

Ty grunted and fisted his hand in her hair while he buried his nose in the damp strands on the other side of her head. A low groan escaped his lips as he came, his hips pinning her to the bed with each ramming thrust.

With her own orgasm subsiding, Evan let go of her shins and locked her ankles at the base of Ty's back. She held on, holding him as close as she could until his movements stopped.

Evan was amazed at the intensity of their lovemaking. Sweat coated their skin. Ty's heart thundered against her chest as she lowered her legs and tangled them with his.

She didn't know what to expect once the tide of sheer ecstasy settled between them. But it felt so good just to lie there entangled in each other. Ty laid his forehead on her shoulder as he pressed himself even deeper inside her.

"That was amaz—"

Ty's lips covered hers, cutting off her words. He kissed her until she lost track of her train of thought. When she sighed against his mouth, he withdrew from her body and rolled over onto his side. Wrapping his arm around her waist, he gathered her close and pressed her back against his chest.

Evan didn't mind. As sweaty as they were, she snuggled against his hips. Aligning her legs with his, she laid her hand over his much larger one that now rested on her hip.

He kissed her cheek then spoke next to her ear. "Tomorrow morning I want to know why you lied to me about you being a vet."

She laced her fingers with his. "Only if you tell me what you have against sleeping with virgins."

She felt Ty stiffen behind her for a brief second. "It's not the same thing."

Evan shrugged. She refused to let him evade her question. "Consider it tit for tat."

"You push too far."

She tensed. His tone had changed. He was withdrawing again. She wouldn't let him put up his barrier any more. "You'll be leaving day after tomorrow. Let's just drop it."

His hand flexed on her hip then his grip tightened for a brief second. "The wedding starts at ten tomorrow. We'd better get some sleep."

Evan closed her eyes and inhaled. For now she'd just relish being surrounded by Ty's scent and muscular body. They were perfect physically and she found him intellectually interesting. But neither one of them seemed to be willing to share something deeper about themselves, which was a shame. Ty made her heart sing on so many levels.

TY LISTENED to Evan's tiny snores as she slept. He smiled in the dark and ran his hand down her thigh and back up. She muttered something and then started to roll over onto her belly.

For some reason he couldn't fathom, a feeling of emptiness came over him at the thought of Evan pulling away from him.

He captured her shoulder and rolled her over. Pushing her head on his chest, he lay on his back and gathered her close.

While she slept, Evan naturally settled her head on his shoulder, flinging her arm across his waist and her thigh over his.

He closed his eyes and fought the possessive thoughts that rushed forth. She was his. No man, not Chad, not anyone, would have her.

As much as he wanted to stand on the rooftop and beat his chest marking his territory, he had to face reality. Evan was a very independent woman. She owned her own successful business, and many people depended on her, even if they didn't give her the respectful title of "doctor" that she very much deserved.

She didn't seem to have a need for a man in her life, other than to help her with the whole virginity thing. Why had she lied to him about being a vet? Did she think the discovery would make him want to stick around? That it made her a greater catch?

He stiffened at the insulting thought. But it kind of made sense in a weird sort of way. As a visitor, he was the perfect person to have no-strings-attached sex with. She could get the deed out of the way without any worry of commitment.

That's what he wanted too, wasn't it? Mind-blowing, no-commitment sex. Correction...very long, drawn-out, blue-ball eliciting, sexually frustrating moments that culminated into fan-fucking-tastic sex. He couldn't believe the woman really yanked on his balls! And that she knew running her fingers down his sac and below would send him over the edge. Damn, sex with Evan felt so good. Her sweet body and adventurous nature were the perfect combination, like she was made just for him.

He clenched his teeth and forced the possessive thoughts from his head. He'd learned his lesson about getting emotionally involved. Come Sunday he'd be on a plane back to Maryland.

Then why couldn't he get enough of Evan's natural cinnamon and vanilla scent? he wondered as he buried his nose in Evan's tangled, damp curls and inhaled. His stomach clenched as he realized his own smell now commingled with hers, and damn, it smelled better than good. It smelled...right.

EVAN AWOKE FEELING SEXUALLY FRUSTRATED. All night she'd dreamed of Ty—the way his hands felt on her body, the sensation of his heated skin sliding along hers, his chest pressing against her breasts and his shaft filling her completely. He'd stretched her in so many delicious ways she was surprised she didn't wake swollen and sore. Instead, she awoke throbbing and aching for release.

She lifted her head and was disappointed to see the bed

was empty beside her. When she glanced toward the window and saw the sun had barely begun to rise, she realized Ty must be outside doing his martial arts thing. At least that gave her a few minutes to herself. It would be better if she took the edge off, than for Ty to think she was desperate for his touch again so soon.

Evan rolled onto her back and placed her feet flat on the bed. Closing her eyes, she skimmed her fingers past her breasts down her belly until they tangled in her soft hair between her thighs.

Thoughts of Ty entered her consciousness as the pads of her fingers found her clitoris.

Her heart rate inched upward when she began to massage the tiny sensitive nub.

She let out a small moan once she finally plunged a finger inside her channel. A frustrated sob escaped when she realized nothing would ever feel as good as Ty sliding inside her, his hard heat surrounding her while his rigid, thick cock plunged deep.

She kept up her pace and her sex reacted to the pleasant, if not majorly exciting, stimulation. She began to move her hips, hoping to rid herself of her body's addiction to Ty.

Evan's skin suddenly heated then chill bumps formed. The strangest sensation she wasn't alone washed over her. She opened her eyes to see Ty leaning against the doorjamb, watching her.

His chest was bare and his jeans were unbuttoned at the waist. She noted the distinct outline of his erection against the soft, worn denim.

Ty stared at her bent knee and the thigh that blocked his view. His green gaze locked with hers. He didn't smile, he just inclined his head. She realized what he was saying, "Lower your leg. I want to watch."

She slowly lowered her leg, but instead of staying in the position she was, she rolled over onto her belly, tossed her hair over her shoulder and arched her back. She glanced back at Ty for a brief second before she faced the headboard. She continued to touch herself, but this time she rocked her hips even more. If asked, she wouldn't have been able to put it to words, but there was something incredibly sexy about Ty watching her. She wanted to make sure it was a show he'd never forget.

When the mattress dipped, Evan paused her movements. Her heart hammered at the realization Ty was behind her on the bed. He was so close she felt his heat on her bare buttocks, but she didn't look back.

Ty's fingers feathered across the curve of her spine before his hands slid down her skin to cup her rear. Her pulse raced and her sex throbbed at the sound of his shallow breathing behind her. Placing his hands on her hips, he lifted them higher. She knew he was telling her to rise up on her knees. Evan complied, her body throbbing in anticipation. She let out a ragged breath and waited.

Ty's body heat spread across her spine as he rubbed his thumbs on the side of her buttocks. She realized he was leaning over her. When she felt his erection touch her entrance then begin to slide inside her, Evan closed her eyes in sexual bliss.

"You're pure temptation."

She shivered at his husky words. As her moist channel stretched to accept him, Evan panted out in amusement, "Is that why you called me Eve yesterday?" Coming from Ty, the nickname made her sound sensual and alluring, like a seductress.

"You're too smart for your own good." Ty thrust deep inside her then groaned, pushing his hips flush with hers.

Evan sobbed at the wonderful sensations ricocheting throughout her body. Somehow she managed to respond. "I've been told that a time or two." What an understatement!

Once he was seated fully inside her, Ty put his hands on her waist and slid his fingers up her rib cage until he cupped her breasts. Clasping her breasts in a firm grip, he pulled her to a kneeling position, aligning her body flush with his warm hard chest and muscular thighs.

"All I've thought about was sinking inside you again. Working out with a hard-on is *not* comfortable."

Evan chuckled at the frustration in his tone. He smelled of outdoors and musk—sexy and so very virile. She was glad to know this out-of-control desire thing hadn't died with the new day upon them. If anything it seemed the rising sun only intensified how she felt about Ty, which scared her a little. She knew he didn't like Texas. Boone was her home and always would be.

Refusing to think beyond the moment, she tilted her head as he planted a kiss on her shoulder. She ran a hand along the firm muscles on his thigh. "At least we're on the same wavelength."

"Good, I'd really hate to think you didn't want me to join in," Ty purred next to her ear.

"Active participation is definitely encouraged."

Ty chuckled at her comeback. He nipped at the soft spot between her shoulder and her neck then slid his hands to her waist. "Bend over, baby."

Evan placed her hands on the headboard. She cast Ty a seductive smile over her shoulder before she used her hold on the headboard to allow her to bend over as far as she could.

"Inventive."

She smiled at the admiration in Ty's tone as she tightened her grip on the headboard and flexed her inner walls around his erection. "Just trusting this will be an experience I won't soon forget."

Ty palmed her hips and growled low in his throat when her walls contracted around him again. "Easy, sweetheart. Give me a chance to move."

Evan pushed back against him, forcing him even deeper inside her. She moaned at the satisfying sensation. "Then by all means..."

Ty withdrew then slowly slid back inside.

Evan clenched her jaw at her body's reaction to the unique position. Chill bumps formed on her skin.

He pulled out and pushed back in once more. When he began to rock while he was partway inside her, Evan's arms and legs started to tremble at the pleasure his movements caused. "God, Ty. I'm...I mean...that feels so good."

"I want you to feel even more," he said as he flattened the palm of his hand against her lower belly. Ty pushed the hand on her belly toward her spine at the same time he thrust forcefully inside her again and again. Evan realized the reason he wasn't ramming deep. He knew the position allowed his cock to hit her hot spot with just the right friction. When Ty's fingers slowly brushed against her clitoris, Evan let out a long mewling wail.

Her orgasm raced through her in a series of rapidly building jolts of pleasure. The pressure from his hand only intensified the body-rocking sensations clamoring inside her. Her belly knotted, her heart raced and her body tensed as her climax built to its highest peak. The intense ecstasy that splintered along her insides made her gasp. Evan clenched her walls and rocked into him as her orgasm spiraled its way throughout her entire body.

When the last contraction subsided, Evan pulled herself up to an upright position and used her hold on the bed as leverage to push back against each of Ty's aggressive thrusts. This time she clenched her muscles, making it more difficult for him to withdraw.

Ty stopped moving for a second and laid his head on her shoulder. He exhaled in harsh bellows. "God you've got a helluva grip, baby."

Evan grinned as she let go of her pelvic muscles then quickly gripped him once more. Ty shuddered against her back. When she finally relaxed her channel, Ty clasped her hips and pulled his erection completely out of her, then slammed back inside her again and again. "Tyyyyyy," she cried out. The hard pressure sent her right over the edge into a second, deeply satisfying climax.

"You feel so damn good." Ty gripped her breasts and held her back tight against his chest as he ground his hips against her rear. He was so deep inside her that when he came, Evan felt each explosive pulse. The intimate sensation sent warmth tingling throughout the rest of her body.

Ty's movements slowed until his body was flush with hers. Heat emanated between them as he slid his right hand under her left breast. Without a word he tucked his hand right up against her thundering heart. Using his hold, he pulled her tight and kissed a path along her neck until he reached her ear. "Whose heart do you think is beating faster?"

Evan felt the heavy thud of his heart hammering against her back. She closed her eyes and placed her hand over his on her heart. Taking a steadying breath, she said, "They're beating at the same jackhammer rate."

The low, sexy growl next to her ear sent a thrilling shiver down her spine, but his next words blew her away. "That's because we're evenly matched."

10

E van sat in her chair watching Ty walk a radiant Jena down the aisle between the rows of white chairs with purple flowers and white bows tied to the "aisle" side. Her father sat to her right and Ty's mother and uncle sat to her left. She felt very self-conscious when Ty introduced her to his mom as the town's veterinarian, especially since Lily chose that moment to walk past them in her perfectly tailored navy suit and her silky black hair pulled up in a French twist. Not a single wisp escaped.

Lily was the epitome of sophistication. The woman oozed confidence with every step she took. Evan had plucked nervously at the skirt of her simple lavender rayon sundress while Ty introduced her to his mother. Evan had to resist the urge to wipe her sweaty palm on her dress before she put her hand out to shake Karen Hudson's hand. But Ty's mother just smiled and shook her hand as if she'd never been happier to meet her.

Karen's green eyes and short dark hair favored Ty's overall

coloring, but Evan could see where Jena inherited her mother's friendly nature. When Mrs. Hudson asked Evan and her father to sit next to her and her brother-in-law during the wedding, Evan quickly came to the conclusion Mrs. Hudson was a gracious and generous woman.

Evan's gaze locked on Ty's handsome form as he handed his sister off to his Uncle Rick and then moved to stand behind Harm's best man.

When the pastor began the wedding ceremony, Evan's gaze remained on Ty. He looked so incredibly handsome in his expensive black business suit, she'd had a hard time keeping her hands to herself when he got dressed for the wedding. On the way to Harm's ranch, Ty told her his sister had insisted on no tuxedos for the groomsmen since Harm and she were marrying outside and they wanted the wedding to be a fun, informal affair.

Ty's broad shoulders filled out his suit to perfection and his starched white shirt made his skin look even darker. He'd really picked up a nice tan during his short stay in Boone, she thought with a half-jealous smirk as she glanced at her bare arms' peachy skin tone. Her skin never turned dark. Instead, it only turned a golden color when she worked outside for extended periods of time.

Evan took a quick glance back through the three-hundred-plus guests who were in attendance at the wedding. Her gaze caught Chad's, who sat diagonally back a few rows. Or his caught hers, rather.

Chad tilted his head her way as a big, broad grin spread across his face.

He pointed to her and then himself, winking as he mouthed, "Dance."

Evan turned around without acknowledging him. Damn, she'd forgotten she'd told him she'd dance with him at the wedding reception. She bit her lip, wondering how she was going to get out of that. If Chad danced like a normal man she wouldn't have an issue. But Chad always danced close, while his hands did a dance all their own. If Ty saw that... She grimaced at the thought of being the cause of another scene. The good news was there were a lot of guests at this wedding. Since she wore flats, she should be able to get lost in the general crowd pretty easily.

She happened to look at Ty at that moment and that's when she saw Ty's gaze had zeroed in on Chad. Though his expression remained impassive, Evan could tell by the direct look in his eyes, he was challenging Chad. As much as the possessive look on Ty's face made her heart sing when he cast his gaze her way, it also made her stomach tense. She vowed to avoid Chad until Ty was finished with his groomsman duties.

———

EVAN GRABBED a glass of wine off a waiter's tray as he passed by. "Thanks," she mumbled before she ducked behind a huge potted plant the florist had brought to hide each of the huge white tent's four corner posts. Taking a sip, Evan swallowed and leaned against the pole. Dodging Chad for the last half-hour had taken a lot of physical dexterity and effort on her part. Damn, she was exhausted.

"Evan, love, there you are," Chad called out as he rounded the other side of the plant. "Remember, you promised—"

"Okaaaaay, let's open a space on the dance floor, everyone. Now's the time for all the bachelors to gather together. Harm's going to throw the garter," Mrs. Hudson's voice came through the mic as the song ended.

Relief washed over Evan at the interruption. She grinned at Chad. "Better get going, Chad. You're still single."

Chad waved her comment away, but at that moment Jena called out from the stage, "You, too, Chad."

Everyone turned and called his name. "C'mon, Chad, m'boy. Get up there," his father bellowed from across the tent.

Chad thrived on attention, especially large crowds. He gave the whole group a huge smile and waved to them as he walked away from Evan to join the single men who'd gathered on the dance floor near the stage.

Harm was up on the stage on bent knee in front of his new wife. A huge grin spread across his face when the catcalls began as he grasped his wife's ankle under her long wedding gown, then slowly slid his hands up her leg, seeking the garter.

When his hand went well past her knee, he tilted his head in surprise and asked, "How far up does this garter go, darlin'?"

The crowd all laughed at his comment while Jena grinned and bent forward to whisper something in his ear.

"Now that she's got me all hot and bothered she tells me it's on the other leg," Harm mock-complained to the crowd. Among uproarious laughter and even more catcalling, Harm moved his hands to Jena's other leg, shaking his head at his wife's sense of humor.

Conversation buzzed around her as Evan watched Harm remove Jena's garter. When he stood up and held his prize aloft on one finger, Evan immediately looked for Ty. Was he among the men who waited to catch the garter?

When she saw him on the fringes of the group of men, as if he only stood there because he had to since he was a groomsman, she couldn't help but feel a bit disappointed. She knew what tradition said the garter symbolically meant...the one who caught the garter would marry next. Is that why Ty didn't seem to want to join in?

Harm turned his back to the crowd and tossed the garter over his head. It sailed through the air until one very determined male hand reached out above all others and grasped the blue and white material in a tight fist. Chad came down from his jump in the air with a triumphant smile on his face.

As she watched the other single men clap Chad on the back in congratulations, Evan exhaled. Good. Chad would be busy for a little while at least.

Her neck tingled and she instinctively knew she was being watched. She turned to see Ty standing beside her.

"Hey," he simply said, but the intensity in his gaze as it slowly moved down her body then back to her face left her feeling as if the world had frozen around them.

"Hey yourself." She took a sip of her wine and tried to act nonchalant. Ty didn't need to know just how much he affected her. No one who was leaving tomorrow should affect her this much, damn it.

Ty reached up and cupped the back of her neck. Her stomach tumbled when he rubbed his thumb along her jaw line.

"I'm sorry I haven't been around."

She smiled. "I understand it's the groomsman's duty to 'work' the party."

Ty gave a sexy smile. "I'll do my best to make sure at least one guest has a great time." He began to pull her closer when his mother's voice came across the mic once more.

"Okay, all you single ladies. Now it's your turn to grab for the golden ring...well, in this case Jena's bouquet. Come on. Gather around."

Ty wrapped his arm around Evan and kissed her temple before he gave her a push. "Get going, sassy. There's a bouquet with your name on it."

Evan grinned. As she walked away, she said, "For once my height just might come in handy."

Ty winked and called after her, "Elbow throwing is illegal."

"I'll keep that in mind." Evan felt on top of the world. Just those few moments alone with Ty put a bounce in her step as she made her way to stand among the group of single women waiting for Jena to throw her bouquet.

"I heard Jena's right-handed, so my guess is since she'll be throwing over her head to us the flowers will go toward the left."

"You strategize too much, Sam. Just grab the damn thing," the other lady next to her said.

Evan shook her head at the two dark-haired ladies in their early thirties who stood in front of her discussing their tactics. They had their plans of capturing the bouquet down to a science.

Harm stood behind Jena as she waved to the group of women. "Hi, ladies. Are you ready?"

"Yes!" everyone called in unison.

Evan didn't plan to get involved in the fun but everyone's enthusiasm around her was so infectious. She called out "yes" along with everyone else as her heart rate picked up in excitement.

Jena smiled and turned her back to the crowd. "One, two,

three," she said right before she launched the bouquet over her head.

The purple and white floral bouquet made a high arc in the air before it zoomed straight down into Evan's hands.

Evan stood there dumbfounded as the crowd applauded and called out, "Evan, Evan, Evan!"

She even laughed when she heard a loud, "Yeehaw!" But her laughter turned into a gasp of disappointment when Chad barreled through the crowd, yelling, "Evan's next to get hitched and so am I." At the same time he grasped her around the waist. Throwing her over his shoulder, Chad played right into the uproarious laughter around them. "Guess we'd better have our fun while we can. Right, folks?"

Everyone laughed and more than a few men yelled out, "Hell yeah!"

"Very funny," Evan mumbled from her upside-down position facing Chad's back.

When Chad headed off the dance floor and straight toward the edge of the tent, apprehension tensed her stomach. "You can let me down now," she said in as low a voice as she could.

Ty narrowed his eyes as he watched the bullshit excuse Chad concocted to capture Evan's attention. The prick knew she wouldn't cause a scene in what appeared to be a good-natured joke. But Ty saw the way Chad's arm tightened around Evan's thighs when he walked off the dance floor. As the arrogant cowboy headed to the side of Harm's ranch home, as if he planned to continue toward the front, Ty felt a tight pain in his chest. When Chad's hand cupped Evan's ass right as he turned out of sight, Ty clenched his jaw. He was done!

He'd taken all of five steps when a heavy hand landed on his arm.

"I don't want to have to arrest anyone today."

Ty cut his sharp gaze to the person who dared stop his exit and was surprised he was staring into Sheriff Master's intense gaze.

"Am I clear?"

Ty shrugged. "Then Chad better not do anything worth getting arrested over."

As soon as Jake let go of Ty's arm, Chad came barreling around the side of the house riding a horse. Evan sat across his lap. Her legs dangled down the horse's left side as she grasped Chad's shoulders tight.

"Yeeeeehaw!" Chad yelled as the horse thundered toward them. The crowd clapped and laughed at his antics.

Ty cast a murderous gaze the sheriff's way. Before he could speak, something hit him on the side of his head as the horse pounded past them.

Ty's heart jerked at the impact, but he recovered and captured the assault weapon before it fell to the ground. He was holding Jena's bouquet.

"Hold that for me!" Evan called out.

Ty's gaze locked with Evan's annoyed one as she shifted her gaze to Chad and rolled her eyes.

Biting, possessive anger, unlike anything he'd ever experienced in his life, spread through him like wildfire. He turned and started to walk toward the side of the house, his shoulders and back tense, already mentally preparing to defend his woman.

"Hold up, son."

Ty stopped walking, ready to explode if the sheriff tried to tell him to stay out of it.

Jake's stare narrowed on Chad's retreating back as the horse took off toward the open pastures behind Harm's home. "I've done some checking on you," he started to say.

Ty set his jaw. He was about to give the man a piece of his mind, when the sheriff continued, "I'll bet with your skills you can do some damage without any physical evidence, can't you?"

Tense shoulders relaxing, Ty gave the sheriff a deadly smile. "Only in defense."

The sheriff squinted after the horse and flicked his tongue over his teeth. Fatherly protection emanated from him as he crossed his arms. "Looks to me like my daughter needs some defending."

ONCE THEY WERE out of sight, Chad slowed the stolen horse to a trot.

Evan scowled. "Very funny. You can take me back now."

Chad's arm tightened around her waist. "No can do, honey." He glanced down at her. "You owe me a dance, remember?"

She was already annoyed with Chad for absconding with one of Harm's horses. The horse was saddled and tied up in the stables. Someone had worked hard tying streamers of purple and white ribbons to the saddle horn. Chad was starting to piss her off.

"Fine. The music and the dance floor are back under the tent."

"Where you'll try to avoid me the rest of the wedding." He shook his head. "Nuh-uh, woman. You promised. You're paying up." He lowered his head and nuzzled her neck. "I guess I'll just have to sing to you for the background music."

"And just how do you expect me to dance with you while I have my hands clapped over my ears?"

Chad smirked as he pulled the horse to a stop. "Nice try, but you're not getting out of it." When he finished speaking, he moved his legs back a little and set her on the saddle. Evan gripped the top of the saddle horn and prayed the horse didn't move while Chad jumped down or she'd be kissing the grass.

Before she had a chance to turn and sit astride, Chad gripped her waist. She'd have done so, even in her dress, just to get back to the wedding. Evan ground her teeth and placed her hands on Chad's shoulders to steady herself while he lifted her down. Once her feet hit the ground, she let go and took a step back. "I know what you're really after, Chad. You may as well give up, because it isn't going to happen."

Chad gripped her waist once more and yanked her close. "Why? Is it because of that Yank? He'll be leaving tomorrow, but I'll always be here, Evan. Boone is our home. You just need to give me a chance." His grip tightened on her waist.

Chad had deliberately made her face facts. Ty would leave tomorrow. Gone. Back to his home and his business in Maryland, and all she'd be left with was memories of their time together. She'd never been so angry in her life. As Chad lowered his mouth to hers, she tried to shove him back, but he grasped her shoulders and planted his lips on hers in a hard kiss.

Evan felt nothing when Chad tried to deepen the kiss. Other than anger. That emotion definitely ran rampant through her mind. Pulling her mouth away from his, she leaned back and whacked him in the nose. Hard.

"Ow!" Chad yelled as he stumbled back and held his hand to his nose. Then he turned his blood-streaked palm toward her. "Shit! I think you just broke my nose."

Evan crossed her arms and shrugged, unapologetic. "That'll teach you to take 'no' as a 'no'."

His eyes widened in disbelief as he covered his nose once more. "But you didn't say 'no'."

"Oh, so me trying to shove you back was a 'yes' in your book?"

"No. I mean...yes. Hell, woman, you're trying to confuse me."

"I'm not trying to confuse you. I'm finally saying what you apparently couldn't figure out on your own. Not every woman wants you Chad. I'm *not* interested. Now, lean forward."

"Huh?"

Evan turned at the sound of a horse's hoof beats approaching fast. "I said, lean forward. Don't tilt your head back or you might swallow the blood. Pinch your nose, too. It'll stop the bleeding faster." Her heart leapt at the sight of Ty galloping toward them on the back of one of Harm's stallions. The man leaned into the horse like he'd been born in the saddle. He'd ditched his jacket and tie and had unbuttoned his collared shirt, but in her mind, nothing was sexier than seeing Ty riding in to save her in his wedding garb and a huge purple and white floral wreath swaying around the horse's neck. The sight of the flowers made her stomach tense. Those purple and white ribbons on the horse Chad stole definitely had a purpose.

The ground shook beneath her feet until Ty stopped his horse a few feet away.

"Need a ride, ma'am?"

She noted the smirk of amusement that lit in Ty's green gaze when he glanced at Chad and saw the man's predicament.

Evan walked over and put her hand in Ty's outstretched one. As he helped her up to sit sideways on the saddle in front of him, Chad called out in a nasal voice as he continued to pinch his nose, "I can take Evan back."

Ty wrapped his arms around Evan's waist and nudged his horse forward until they stood beside the horse Chad had taken.

Leaning over, he grabbed the other horse's reins and started to turn both horses around.

"Wait! You can't leave me here. I need a ride."

Evan felt Ty's body tense behind her. "I'm taking both horses. They were waiting to be Harm and Jena's ride away from their wedding reception."

"Oh no," Evan whispered at Ty's confirmation of her concerns about the decorated saddle horn on the horse Chad took. Chad might've been the one who stole the horse, but embarrassed heat still rode her cheeks as Ty began to trot away with the horses.

When they reached the stables, Ty's arm tightened around Evan's waist and his lips moved close to her ear. "I've never wanted to flatten someone as much as I did that asshole. I hate to admit it, it's probably a good thing you took care of him."

Evan sighed. "Setting Chad straight was long overdue."

Ty slid his nose along her neck, then spoke in her ear. "Since you're in a forthcoming mood, I want to know why you didn't tell me you were a vet."

Evan turned to look up at him. Heat arced between them. "Only if you tell me—"

Ty's lips landed on hers. Her heart raced at the intensity of his kiss. Evan reached up and touched his jaw. She opened her mouth under his, wishing they were alone for more than a brief few minutes. She had a feeling someone would come looking for them soon.

Ty pulled his mouth away and stared down into her eyes, waiting for her to answer.

Evan returned his heart-stopping stare. For several seconds her pulse pounded in her ears. Did she really want to open up to Ty? To tell him one of her biggest insecurities. His hand moved from her waist to her thigh and squeezed. Not a word was spoken, but she realized from that one touch her trust seemed very important to him.

Evan started to speak when a familiar booming voice interrupted her.

"Evelyn! There you are."

Her father walked up to the horse and put his hands in the air to help her down. Evan cast an apologetic look Ty's way before she put her hands on her father's shoulders and allowed him to lower her to the ground.

"Hey, Dad."

Her father looked up at Ty as he put his arm around her shoulders. "No arrests?"

Ty shook his head.

"What are you two talking about?" Evan asked as her

father steered her out of the stables and back toward the festivities.

Jake chuckled. "Nothing. Just men-speak."

Ty's hand fisted around the reins as he watched Evan walk away with her father. Evan was the most independent woman he'd ever met. Despite the fact her father was the town sheriff and overprotective to boot, he had a feeling she'd skipped the crawling stage and went straight to walking on her own two feet just as soon as her legs would hold her weight.

He should be relieved he didn't have to kick the shit out of Chad—everything his aikido training had ingrained in him focused on self-defense only, that he should never take the aggressive offensive. But he wasn't relieved. Instead, seeing the evidence Evan had taken care of herself caused his male pride to take a hit.

Frustration built inside him like a storm brewing to full throttle fury. Why he felt this way, he didn't have a damned clue. All he knew was he wanted to see Evan's vulnerable side. Hell, he wanted to know she had one. If nothing else, he wanted her to trust him enough to tell him why she'd lied to him.

He climbed off his horse and retied both horses' reins back to their posts to await the bride and groom.

Ty clasped Evan's hand tight and tugged her up the stairs and into the Double D ranch house. She followed him, unsure of his quiet mood. After she'd walked away with her father from the stables, Ty had had more wedding duties to fulfill, so they didn't see each other again until Harm and Jena rode off at the end of the wedding reception.

"Ty, what is it?" She tried to get a response from him, but he remained stoic.

When he tossed his jacket on the back of the couch, then walked into the bedroom, she let him tug her along until he pulled her into the bathroom and shut the door behind them, Evan pulled out of his hold, her chest tightening with apprehension. "What's wrong?"

Ty flipped on the shower then turned her around. When he unzipped the back of her dress, then moved his fingers to the straps on her shoulders, Evan held onto the scraps of material before he could pull them down her arms.

She cast a serious look over her shoulder. "Talk to me or these clothes aren't coming off."

Ty's hooded gaze remained on hers as he let go of her straps and began to unbutton his own shirt. Evan couldn't resist. She turned to face him while he shrugged out of the cotton shirt. Broad, tan shoulders, a mouthwatering chest and cut abs she'd never get tired of seeing surfaced as his shirt landed in a heap on the floor. Evan had to press her lips together to keep the anger she felt in the forefront of her mind.

Heat began to fill the room. Steam hung in the air around them, a physical veil coating the sexual tension that vibrated between them.

Ty's fingers moved to her straps once more. Evan's breathing turned shallow. The man literally made her ache and he'd yet to touch her. She was so caught up in his deep green gaze she let her hands fall to her sides.

When her dress slid down her body to pool at her feet, Ty's line of sight lowered to her bare breasts as he pulled the bowstring untying one side of her underwear, then the other.

Evan's gaze followed the filmy black material until it fluttered to land on top of her dress. She realized that underwear was the only sexy piece of underclothing she owned. She'd have to remedy that sad situation soon. Her heart raced when Ty's fingers lightly brushed the strawberry-blonde curls between her legs.

He hooked a finger under her chin and applied pressure until her gaze met his once more. "You trust me to take away your clothes—a physical protection of your body. I want you to trust me enough in your heart to tell me the truth."

Evan's chest lurched. Each time they were together, the man dug a little deeper into her heart. She knew if she opened up to him, it would hurt so much more when he left, but she'd never felt so close to another person. It just felt right to share with this incredible, complex man, but she'd do it her way.

She smiled as she unbuckled his belt, and then unbuttoned and unzipped his dress pants. "You sure know how to get right to the heart of things, don't you?"

As she hooked her thumbs on the waistband of his boxers, a warning tone entered Ty's voice, "Evan."

Evan pushed his boxers down his thighs, kissing her way down his abdomen.

Ty's stomach muscles flexed underneath her lips. His fingers shot through her hair when she let his boxers fall the rest of the way down to his ankles so she could blow her hot breath across his erection.

"Evan, stop trying to distract me."

She smiled at the tension in his tone, then ran her tongue

from the base of his erection all the way to the tip in a slow, leisurely lick. "There's no distraction going on, Ty. Just a two-way street." She straightened and faced him. "I don't plan on venturing down it alone."

Ty's fingers curled in her scalp, his touch tense, possessive...affected. He pulled her flush against his body, his lips a breath away from hers. Her stomach tightened at the exhilarating sensation of his hard cock pressed against her lower belly and the coiled tension in his muscular arms around her.

"Why do you always challenge me?"

The mix of emotions churning in his eyes surprised her. Evan stood on her toes and pressed a soft kiss to his lips. "Because you need it."

THE TRUTH of Evan's words pierced right to his heart, making his chest constrict. Not only did he have to have the sexual attraction, but he needed the stimulating banter. He wanted a woman who gave as good as she got, yet deep in his heart he also needed a woman who gave him as high a priority as he did her. Lily had definitely left her mark on him. She'd taught him what he didn't want in a woman.

Ty lifted Evan in his arms and stepped under the warm, hard shower spray. Setting her on her feet, he grasped her back then lowered his mouth to her breast, capturing the nipple. He sucked hard on the sensitive nub until Evan's fingers tightened in his hair.

She arched and moaned, clutching him closer. Ty nipped at the pink tip and moved his hands lower to clasp her sweet rear.

The sensation of the water sluicing over them and her soft

skin rubbing against his erection made him throb to be inside her as soon as possible.

He kissed his way to her other breast and applied the same attention. "Tell me, Evan," he mumbled before he rolled her nipple between his teeth.

Evan's breath came out in short, rapid pants as her fingers grasped the muscles along his hips. "Not...fair."

Ty slid his hand down her belly to her mound while he rubbed his five o'clock shadow across her nipple, swollen from his kisses. "I never claimed to be a fair man."

Evan grabbed his balls. He shuddered at her touch and the fact her aggression turned him on even more.

She slowly trailed her fingers up his cock. "All's fair..." she shot back.

He chuckled. The woman yanked his chain better than any female he'd ever been with.

"My IQ ranges from 160 to 170 depending on what IQ test I've been given."

Ty met her gaze, surprised by her statement. Before he could speak, she continued, "I went to college when I was sixteen and had my vet's license and MBA by time I turned twenty-four." She grimaced. "Let's just say, growing up the sheriff's daughter, combined with the ability to spin intellectual circles around men, was a turn-off in the relationship department, except to Chad, apparently." She shrugged. "From past experience...well, that's why I lied."

Ty gathered her close and buried his nose in her neck. "Your ability to improvise and adapt has impressed me both intellectually and sexually, and I'm sure as hell not intimidated by your dad."

Evan laughed as she slid her hands across his broad shoulders. "I definitely think we're on the same page in the pleasure department."

"But there is one thing..."

SHE RAISED HER EYEBROWS, waiting for him to continue.

"You've worked hard for your doctorate. You deserve the respect you've earned. Don't be afraid to ask for it just because you started off younger than your peers."

Her stomach tensed. "What are you talking about? My patients respect my judgment."

Ty shook his head and gave a half-smile. "I can tell they respect you, but have you noticed none of them call you Doctor Masters?"

Evan laughed his comment off. She had noticed, but gave up worrying about it. "That's because they've all known me since I was a kid. They saw me hanging around Doc Peterson's veterinary office all the time, watching him do his job. He retired the year I got my vet's license." She smiled at the memory. "Said he was just waiting on me to finish up my schoolin' so he could leave his animals in good hands."

Ty's dark eyebrows drew downward. "You've earned that title, Evan."

Evan grinned as she began to tickle his waist. "And *you* need to loosen up and laugh a lot more."

Ty grabbed her hands and held them captive. "Stop that."

The warm water beat down on them, bouncing off their shoulders in tiny spatters as she met his serious gaze. "Why? Because you'll laugh? What's wrong with being silly?" she asked as she began to slide her slippery foot up his leg.

Ty's lips twitched as if he were trying not to fall victim to her antics.

Evan grinned. "Oooh, I think he's about to laugh. As a matter of fact, I predict a deep-bellied guffaw coming."

Ty laughed outright, then flashed a brilliant smile. It was the kind of smile that was so engaging, it startled Evan. The man might be handsome as hell with his intense, brooding persona, but he damn near bowled her over when he turned on the charm. Her heart swelled that this was the first genuine happy-go-lucky smile she'd seen since she met him and she'd had a part in bringing it out. "Now it's your turn."

He raised a dark eyebrow. "My turn?"

"To share."

Ty NODDED and pulled her close until she laid her head on his shoulder. "When I was seventeen I fell in love. The girl was the first woman I had sex with. I was her first as well." He sighed heavily, remembering the pain Lily's words had caused. "Let's just say, after a whole summer together, she didn't think I was the man for her."

Evan's chest tightened to hear the heartbreak in Ty's voice. She wrapped her arms around his trim waist and hugged him tight. "Was Lily that woman?" she asked in a quiet voice.

Ty's body tensed for a second before he cupped the back of her head and ran his fingers down her wet hair. "Yeah. She thought pursuing her professional aspirations was more important than us, that I would only hold her back."

The tone of his voice made Evan's stomach tense. No wonder he had a thing against sleeping with virgins. It wasn't what he'd originally told her—that he thought the woman would expect some kind of commitment from the act, but that *he* had thought being Lily's first had meant more in their relationship. In the end, Lily had chewed him up and spit him out.

Evan had heard her girlfriends talk about their first love... that they'd never forget them. She knew she'd never forget Ty. What had started out as a convenient means to an end had turned into so much more. She realized she'd fallen in love with this deeply intense, fiercely protective yet surprisingly tender man. She'd never forget their time together. Ever.

When she inhaled, her heart actually ached, but she had to know how Ty felt about Lily after all this time. "Do you still love her?"

Ty stopped stroking her hair. A long heart-stopping moment passed before he answered.

"No."

Relief spread through her. She slowly exhaled the breath she'd been holding.

Tension filled the air between them. She didn't want Ty's last night in Texas to be filled with sad thoughts. She wanted him to stay, but he hadn't said anything to indicate he felt deeper feelings for her beyond their physical attraction. Plus, he had a business to run back in Maryland. The least she could do, as a thank you for him fulfilling her request, was to send the man off with happier memories of Boone.

Picking up the bar of soap, she cast him a wicked grin. "You know, ever since I saw you in the shower, I've been dying for a repeat performance. Only this time, I want to stay until the finale."

Ty flashed her a rakish grin as he took the soap and ran it along her palm. Her heart thundered as he set the soap back on the dish then guided her hand to his erection, where he slowly wrapped her soapy fingers all the way around him.

Bending close, he kissed her neck at the same time he cupped her mound in a dominant, possessive hold. As he slid a finger deep in her channel, the low, rumbling register of his voice sent intense excitement straight to her toes. "How about this time we're both intimately involved in the pleasurable ending."

THE SENSATION of warm lips pressing against her temple woke Evan. Ty's soap and masculine scent surrounded her. She inhaled, then stretched and smiled.

"Morning, Doc."

Her eyes flew open at the nickname. When her morning eyes focused on his clean-shaven face and damp hair, Evan's heart jerked. It was Sunday. He was leaving at some point today. She sat up on her elbow and took in his dark heather-green T-shirt and faded blue jeans.

"Where are you going, good-lookin'?" She tried her best to sound as casual as possible, even though her heart was already breaking into tiny pieces.

Ty ran his hand down her hair and cupped her chin. She liked the tiny lines that formed around his eyes when he smiled. They told her what she already knew. Ty smiled more often than he let on. "My mom wanted me to join my uncle and her for breakfast with Harm and Jena before the newly-weds left for their honeymoon."

Relief flooded through her, relaxing the tension that had stiffened her shoulders. Yesterday, after their shower and a quick dinner, Ty had carried her to bed and kept her up until the wee hours, taking her to new sexual highs. Her body might ache in a bone-deep I-couldn't-get-enough-of-this-man-so-I'm-going-to-pay-for-it-later kind of way, but she'd never regret one single moment she'd spent with Ty.

"What time is your flight?"

"Two." Ty leaned forward and brushed his lips against hers before he whispered in her ear, "The well-tumbled look suits you."

Heat rose to her cheeks when Ty's intense gaze met hers once more.

"Damn, I wish I hadn't promised I'd meet my family for breakfast."

She grinned then lay down on her back and stretched like a languorous cat, pressing her naked breasts against the thin sheet covering her body. "I guess I'll just lounge around in bed all day then."

"Don't tempt me," Ty growled as he stood. He glanced at his watch. "It's nine now. I should be back in an hour and a half. Will you still be here?"

Evan laughed and answered truthfully. "Yes, recovering."

Ty chuckled and started to leave the bedroom. But he turned back, a quizzical expression on his face. "I'm curious. You're obviously an animal lover, but since you've spent a few days here I have to assume you don't have any pets at home to take care of. Why don't you have any pets of your own?"

Evan leaned on her elbow, surprised by his question about her personal life. "As you know I'm pretty much on-call all the time. It wouldn't be fair to have a pet I don't get to spend much time with. And my yard is very small. I'd want to have more land for my pets." She lifted her lips in a half-smile and shrugged. "One day. For now, I look at it this way...I have a whole practice full of pets."

Ty nodded his understanding, then kissed her once more before he turned and left the bedroom.

Once he'd driven away, she got out of bed and stretched every protesting muscle in her body. *A shower...that's what I need. The heat will help loosen my muscles.* She headed for the bathroom whistling an uplifting tune.

She had at least an hour with Ty before he had to leave. When he got back, she wasn't going to dwell on the leaving part, but enjoy every last minute of the here-and-now part.

Ty's MIND shifted through thoughts in rapid succession as he turned his car and headed up the dirt road that led to the Double D ranch. He'd never felt so free and excited in all his thirty-six years, all because of a woman who knew how to enjoy life to its fullest, a woman whom he was drawn to on many levels, a woman he just couldn't get enough of. Evan was everything he wanted. Everything that mattered. She was dedicated, generous, sassy and...independent.

That last descriptive word struck him hard. Evan was incredibly self-sufficient. Would she want someone like him in her life—a man with a protective streak a mile wide—for more than a weekend? For that matter, what *did* he want from this? He'd never expected the young veterinarian to turn his heart inside out, or that having mind-blowing sex with Evan would meld into true love making. But that's what he'd done last night. Even if she wasn't aware, he'd made love to Evan. Had she felt the difference in him?

He didn't want to open his heart up again, to leave himself

vulnerable for the kind of heartbreak that took him at least a decade to overcome. His feelings for Evan ran so much deeper than they had for Lily. Lily didn't make him shudder when her fingers grazed his skin. He'd laughed a lot back then, but Lily didn't try to see beyond his laughter to his insecurities. She didn't look that deep.

Evan bowled right through his carefully erected emotional barriers. With her infectious smile and upbeat personality, she made him look at himself, see he was being an ass and showed him how to laugh again. He'd forgotten what it was like to laugh so freely with another. Hell, come to think of it, he hadn't allowed himself the luxury in a very long time.

But he had to face facts. He lived in Maryland and she lived in Texas. What did the future hold for them?

The sight of Evan's SUV coming toward him, dirt kicking up behind her tires, drew him out of his reverie. Ty glanced at his watch to make sure he hadn't somehow run late. No. He was right on time.

He pulled his car over and put on his brakes at the same time Evan did.

"Hey, I saw you left your cell phone behind, so I tried to call Jena, but you'd already left their house. I've got an emergency surgery at my office."

Ty didn't like the sinking feeling that knotted his stomach. He adopted a neutral expression. "How long do you think you'll be?"

Evan's ponytail swished behind her as she shook her head. "I don't know. The cat's pretty mangled from what I understand." She gave him an apologetic smile. "I'm sorry, Ty. I'll call your cell when I get a better idea of the situation, okay?"

Ty clamped his jaw to keep from blurting out, "But I want

you to stay, damn it." He knew it was a selfish reaction, but still one he couldn't help thinking.

"Good luck with the cat." Nodding, he put his foot on the gas pedal and headed toward the house.

EVAN CALLED Ty's cell phone on her way back to the Double D. Tears streamed down her cheeks, her emotions at an all-time high as her vehicle's wheels rumbled over the potholes in the dirt road. After spending a couple of hours trying to repair the damage to the cat, she lost the poor soul anyway. It was the first animal she'd lost during a surgery. The sad experience, coupled with the fact she'd never been able to call Ty to say goodbye made her reaction that much stronger.

When the house came into view and she saw Ty's car was gone, she couldn't hold back the sob that escaped. In her heart, she'd hoped Ty had changed his flight to stay longer so they could say a proper goodbye. His empty parking space told her otherwise.

She'd parked and cut the engine by the time Ty's voicemail came across her cell. Evan closed her eyes and listened to his deep voice, her heart aching.

As the beep sounded, she sniffed back her tears. Ty didn't need to know how upset she was. "Ty, I'm so sorry I wasn't able to call you before you left. The surgery..." she paused and tried to keep her voice from trembling, "it took longer than I anticipated. I wish I'd had a chance to say goodbye. Well, I guess that's what I'm doing now, though I'm finding it hard to come up with the words while speaking to your voicemail. Call me."

Evan punched the Off button, then climbed out of her car. Butterflies flitted in her belly and her hopes picked up at the thought Ty might have left her a note. She shut the car door and strode over to the porch, taking the steps two at a time in her haste to get inside.

As soon as she came through the door, her gaze instantly searched places Ty might have left her a note in the small house.

The sight of a white sheet of paper sitting on the kitchen table made her heart race. Her boot heels sounded loud in the empty house as she hurried over to pick up the note Ty had left her.

Evan,

You know that vet's assistant you pretended to be...have you considered the possibility you might need one.

Ty

Evan's heart felt as if Ty had squeezed it with all his might. The pain was so great her breath came in rampant pants. The note slid out of her fingers and fluttered to the floor as she plopped in one of the chairs, unable to stand on her suddenly shaky legs. Not one word of goodbye. No "I had a good time. Take care". Nothing. Just a curt note, written not in a question form, but as a statement—a statement that basically said she wasn't capable of handling her practice on her own.

11

E van stood in front of the black glass-front cabinet in one of her exam rooms. Clipboard and pen in hand, she'd already checked the other exam rooms' supplies. She could've had her secretary do this task, but she wanted to be absolutely certain all the exam rooms were stocked with all necessary supplies.

It'd been four weeks since Ty had left without a word. He never had returned her phone call. It took her a week and a half to get over the hurt Ty's silence had caused. That's when the realization hit her. Could it be that Ty thought she was just like Lily? A woman who cared only for herself, who put her desires above all else?

No matter how hurt she was by the way Ty had left, his comment in the note he'd left behind had stuck with her. Evan didn't realize she'd allowed her job to become her life the past few years, but the truth was, because of the way she'd grown up—smarter and younger than her peers—she never really did fit in.

The only place she'd felt as if she truly belonged, and was accepted for who she was, was as the town's vet. So she'd thrown herself into her career without taking time out for herself. In the past, it didn't matter. She didn't have anyone else in her life. That was, until she met Ty.

She checked the inventory items off her list and wondered what Ty was doing now. Thoughts of him still made her heart ache.

"See you on Monday, Doctor Masters. I've got Doc Peterson's number written down if I need him," Nicole called out from the front office.

"Goodnight, Nicole...and it's Evan," Evan called back with a sigh. The new vet assistant, Nicole Shannon, she'd hired a couple of weeks ago had insisted on calling her Doctor Masters from day one. Marlene, her secretary, had even joined in this new campaign to the point several of her patients this past week had started calling her Doc Masters. *Wouldn't Ty be pleased?* she thought with a twist of her lips as she set the clipboard down on the counter and finished checking off her list.

Something dropped on the clipboard then bounced to the floor at her feet.

Evan pulled at her prairie skirt to move the calf-length hem out of the way so she could see what had fallen. Her brow furrowed at the blue and white garter that had landed between her boots. She'd seen Chad driving around in his brand-new convertible with that damn garter hanging from his mirror. The couple of times he'd seen her, he'd flicked the garter and raised his eyebrows, as if to say it was only a matter of time before he'd get her to go out with him again. Ugh! She really wasn't in the mood for his games today.

"Chad—"

She tensed at the sound of his boots stepping into her personal space and then froze when he pressed his chest against her back.

Masculine hands landed on the counter on either side of her, caging her in. They weren't Chad's.

"I have this ache that needs tending to and there's only one doctor I want to do the job."

Ty's deep voice made her heart kick up while his masculine scent and body heat enveloped her in a blanket of sensory seduction. Despite her anger at him, she couldn't help the way he made her feel. Her pulse thrummed at a rampant pace, but she replied in an even tone, "I'm sorry, but I'm an animal doctor. I believe Doctor Shelton is taking new patients."

Ty's hands encircled her waist and his warm breath tickled her neck as he bent close to her ear. "I've got the right doctor. I definitely feel animalistic whenever I'm anywhere near you."

Evan's stomach flip-flopped. The man was so damn sexy he made her knees weak. His heat had begun to permeate her white coat while tiny tingling waves of awareness spread from his hands clamped around her waist down to her belly and straight to her core. She closed her eyes against the sensations clamoring inside her.

"Why are you here?" She finally croaked past the lump in her throat.

Ty kissed her neck then nuzzled the soft skin. "Because every day without you was pure torture. You made my pulse race whenever I caught sight of you or inhaled your sweet scent. You made me take a hard look at who I was and to learn to laugh at myself again. Evan, you were the vitality missing from my life. When I'm with you, I feel whole."

His heartfelt confession shredded her. She held back a sob,

but she couldn't hold back the tremor in her voice. "Why didn't you call me?"

Ty turned her around. His green gaze searched hers as he clasped her shoulders. "Because I didn't want to be hurt again. But I realized that you're all I want, and if sharing you with your career was the only way I could be part of your life, then I'd have to come to terms with that."

Tears surfaced as she gripped his chambray shirt. "But you live in Maryland."

The tiny scar above Ty's right eyebrow added a sexy ruggedness to his good looks. His devastating smile made her heart skip several beats. "Actually, I'm renting out the Double D for a few months."

Her stomach clenched. "A few months?"

Ty nodded. "It takes a while to build your dream home if you want to do it right."

Evan swallowed the heart-wrenching emotion that welled up in her throat. "Your dream home?"

Ty unbuttoned the two buttons that held her long white coat closed and slid his hands under her white linen shirt. Sliding his fingers along the smooth skin at her waist, he pulled her close. "*Our* dream home, with plenty of property for animals to run."

The serious intensity in his voice made her legs tremble. Did that mean what she thought it meant?

"That is if you'll consider sharing your life with a man, who'll need to know from time to time that he's still a high priority in your life."

Evan's blood rushed in her ears and her heart thumped at a rapid pace. "Sharing my life? Are you asking me to marry you?"

Ty's white teeth flashed. She loved seeing those crinkles around his eyes once more. "Do you think the sheriff would have it any other way? Though he probably would like our kids to have the 'Masters' last name, I'm a selfish bastard. I want to make sure you're all mine, 'til death do us part."

Evan was completely choked up by Ty's marriage proposal.

Gulping back her emotion, she asked, "You think you can handle me?"

Ty chuckled. "No. I'll probably spend the rest of my life trying though." His gaze turned serious as he finished, "But I'll die a happy man, nonetheless. Will you marry me, Evan?"

Evan narrowed her gaze. "You've got a lot of nerve showing up and asking me to marry you after leaving me like you did."

Sincere regret settled on Ty's features. "I'm sorry if I hurt you by not returning your call, but I knew if I called you, I'd want to see you and the cycle would start all over again. I had to come to terms with myself first. Do you understand that?"

Evan shook her head. "Nope. I'm not the kind of person who just sits and waits for others to come around."

Ty raised his dark eyebrows. His hands tightened around her waist. "What are you saying?"

She moved her nose close to his neck and inhaled. Ty's spicy scent intoxicated her like no other. The man truly had her dangling on a string. Pressing her lips against his jaw, she enjoyed the rough texture of his five o'clock shadow scraping her mouth.

Pulling back a little, she said, "I have a plane to catch in less than two hours."

Ty's jaw ticced as he set her away from him. His hands slid

down to grip her hips in a firm hold. Deep hurt reflected in his dark green eyes. "Who is he?"

Tears shimmered in her eyes, blurring her vision. "I planned to go after the man who taught me to grow up both physically and mentally in a very astute and loving way. I wasn't about to let him slip through my fingers. If he didn't have faith, I had enough for the both of us."

Surprise crossed his features. "You were coming to Maryland?"

Her quick nod sent her unshed tears rolling down her cheeks. "I didn't know what I was going to say to you, but I figured the words would come when I saw you again."

Ty rubbed his thumbs along her cheeks, wiping away her tears. His deep green gaze searching hers. "Do you love me?"

She put her hands over his. "So much it hurts."

Ty pulled her to his chest, wrapping his arms around her in a tight hold. He kissed her hair, then said with a half-laugh, "I'm glad to know I'm in good company."

"Come on, Doc." Reaching for her hand, he tugged her behind him as he made his way out of the exam room. "There's something I've been dying to show you."

Evan's hand tightened around Ty's to slow him down so she could grab her purse from behind the counter. She released his hand long enough to remove her coat and hang it on a hook behind the door. Once she retrieved her keys, she locked her office door, then allowed him to escort her to his car.

As Ty opened the passenger door, Evan smiled at the shiny black Mustang with its convertible top folded down. "Nice car. I'm glad it's a warm day. Did you do a long-term rental for this one?"

Ty shut the door behind her. "No, this one's bought and paid for."

Her surprised gaze followed him as he settled in his seat and started the engine. "When did you buy it?"

"Last week."

Last week? She frowned as he put the car and gear and backed out of the parking lot. "How long have you known you were coming back?"

"Two and a half weeks."

Evan's heart rate elevated with her temper.

"Ow!" Ty jerked his gaze to hers when she punched his arm. "What was that for?"

"For putting me through hell for so long, when you knew you were coming back."

Ty rubbed his muscle as he kept an eye on the road. "I had to talk my partner into working with me on a long-distance basis. Then I had to buy land, buy a car, talk to Jena about renting out the Double D property, take care of clients at work—"

"There's one thing you forgot to do in all your planning," she interrupted him. "You know...something important, like *telling me that you love me and finding out if I felt the same.*"

His gaze snapped to hers, desire burning in their emerald depths. Grasping her hand, he kissed her knuckles. "I loved you from the moment you threw a towel over my head, tied me up and threatened to stick it to me, Doctor Masters. As for you loving me..." He glanced at the road then winked at her. "If I had to, I planned to wear you down until you admitted you loved me just as much."

Happiness radiated through her to finally hear him say those three little words. Leaning back in the leather seat, she put her booted foot on the console between them and pulled her skirt higher, exposing her knee.

"So what is it that you've been dying to show me?"

Ty took his eyes off the road for a second, saw her exposed knee, then jerked his gaze back to hers. His lips tilted in a sexy smile at the same time his hand landed on her knee.

Evan returned his smile as she pulled the clip out of her hair, tossing it in the backseat. Running her fingers through the freed locks, she enjoyed the sensation of the hot Texas wind whipping at her curls.

When Ty's hand slid to her naked thigh and he began to massage the firm muscles, Evan's body ignited. Pulsing heat flooded her lower body, while her heart revved to the point she had to hold back her pants of anticipation.

Ty kept his eyes on the road as he massaged her leg in attentive, seductive circles while slowly moving his hand lower with each rotation.

Evan saw the intent in the brief hooded gaze he cast her way. He planned to draw this out, to make her wait and wait and wait before she exploded. But she had other ideas. She wanted Ty to lose it today, to finally see that primitive side she knew existed just below the surface.

Putting her hand over his, she moved his hand back to her knee. "Where are you taking me?"

Ty turned a raised eyebrow her way when she'd stopped his hand's descent, but he kept his hand where she put it. "Back to our place."

"Ah." Evan trailed her fingers over his, then slid her own fingers down her thigh in a slow, seductive caress.

She watched Ty's reaction out of the corner of her eye. His

gaze darted between the road and her leg so often she realized she was getting equal time.

Evan slipped her hand under her skirt, hoping he imagined her doing all kinds of things to herself. She was already aching. Damn the man for making her want him so much.

"Why are we going back to the Double D?" She tried to sound casual, but the hungry look on Ty's face only made her throb for him even more.

"You'll see." Ty's gaze locked on her skirt-covered lap. His hand tightened on her knee and a muscle jumped in his jaw.

"Come on, share with me." Her voice came out breathless and husky. She closed her eyes to try to focus. Her body was so primed, she was beginning to lose her train of thought.

"Damn straight," Ty uttered as he grasped her wrist then slid his hand over hers. Before she knew what he intended, he pressed both their hands against her entrance. Evan bit her lower lip. Her body wanted desperately to move against the pressure, but instead she held perfectly still, letting the anticipation build inside her.

Ty's lips twisted in a devilish smile as he laced his fingers with hers, then lifted their locked hands to his mouth. While Ty's line of sight returned to the road, his warm tongue encircled her pointer finger, sucking in into his mouth. The action was so erotic and seductive, it ignited a yearning all the way to her core. All she could do was stare in entranced astonishment.

Pulling her finger from his mouth, he pressed a tender kiss to her palm. "I've missed your sweet taste," he said, hungry, lustful arousal reflected in his gaze.

The man left her totally speechless. Once again, he'd turned her attempt to drive him crazy around on her. Would she ever see his unrestrained side? As she glanced at the trees lining the dirt driveway they'd turned down, she'd been so caught up, she didn't realize they were almost to the house.

Ty pulled up to the small ranch house and cut the engine. Without a word, he got out of the car and walked to her side.

Evan sighed as her gaze followed his confident stride. It didn't matter. The man made her shudder at his touch. He made her boneless putty in his hands. She couldn't expect to undo years of mental and emotional barriers overnight. But she had confidence she could break through one day.

Opening the door, he offered his hand to help her out of the car.

Evan put her hand in his.

Ty's grip on her hand felt tight. She had all of a second to glance up at him in surprise before he jerked her forward and used the momentum to toss her over his shoulder.

"Ty!"

When he headed straight toward the barn, she smacked at his jeans-covered butt.

"Hey! What gives?"

Ty closed the stable door behind him and set her booted feet on the hay-strewn ground. Regardless of his enigmatic behavior, Evan's heart rate shot up.

She barely had time to put her hands on his chest before he walked her back against the closed door.

Ty lowered his nose close to her neck and inhaled deeply as he pressed his chest against hers. "I wanted to take my time with you after being apart for so long." He pulled on his belt buckle and yanked at the fly on his jeans as he bellowed in and out in harsh gusts.

Evan's heart hammered at the barely held control emanating from him. Her hands lowered to his waist. "I want to see you let go," she whispered against his neck as she pushed his pants and underwear down his hips, jerking the material past his knees.

Ty's hands were already under her skirt, pushing it higher. His warm fingers slid up the back of her thighs. Gripping her legs, he let out a harsh growl.

Evan moved her hands to his shoulders. Tight muscles flexed underneath the soft chambray material as if Ty were about to explode. She panted, her rampant breathing moving in tandem to the blood whooshing through her body.

Ty nipped at her skin between her shoulder and her throat right before he grasped her buttocks and lifted her thighs around his waist.

Her heart jerked in frenzied excitement when he pressed his erection against her entrance.

"You make me forget everything but being inside you."

She kissed his stubbled jaw and chuckled. "Like the fact I still have on underwear?"

Ty gripped her rear and jerked his hips. The primal action shoved his cock deeper inside her despite the cotton barrier.

"Do you really think a thin piece of material will stop me, sweetheart?"

His husky words and the thong's fragile material standing between them sent her libido skyrocketing.

She knew she could easily shift to the left or right and give him the access he craved, but Ty's intemperate mood was indescribably sexy, his aggressive actions so heart-stoppingly raw and real, she wanted him to find his way through the barrier between them. She needed him to take their relationship to the uninhibited level she knew existed just below the surface.

She kissed his neck. "You're all I've ever wanted."

Ty's mouth slanted over hers in a fierce, possessive kiss as he rammed his erection deeper inside her.

Evan whimpered and rocked her hips. Her belly knotted in anticipation and tears spilled from the corners of her eyes. She throbbed with the need to feel him let go of his steely control, to experience him taking her as hard and as deep as he'd always wanted to.

Ty's hands cupped her rear so tight she was certain she'd have bruises in the shape of his fingers as a reminder of their reunion.

The wood behind her back felt rough, but she didn't care. Her entire body jolted and shuddered with each dominant thrust. *This* was the Ty she'd wanted to experience. He didn't hold back. Instead pure emotion and primal instincts drove him. She'd damn well make sure he never held back from her again.

Evan broke their kiss and wrapped her arms tight around his neck. "Go for it. I'm all yours." She locked her boots together at the base of his back, then lightly bit at the tendon flexing on his throat.

Ty let out a sound she never thought she'd hear from him. The deep, rumbling roar both scared and thrilled her as he ripped right through the fabric separating them.

The sensation of his cock shoving deep inside her sent Evan straight through the roof. She screamed as her orgasm rolled through her in rapid pulsating waves of heart-pounding pleasure.

Ty's knees buckled for a brief second before he caught himself. Then he continued rocking her against the door as he grunted through his own spiraling climax.

His head rested on her shoulder and with each upward

thrust, he groaned and clutched her closer. Through the last few lingering tremors of her orgasm, he didn't withdraw at all. He just let gravity take him as deep inside her as he could go. Evan didn't think Ty had ever been so physically and emotionally connected to another person as he was at that moment.

Her emotions were riding so high, her heart beating so hard, she had to take deep breaths to keep from feeling lightheaded. The only sound that filled the air was their heavy breathing. When Ty pressed a tender kiss to her neck, she whispered in his ear, "Ask me again."

Ty met her gaze, and even in the dim light filtering in the stables, she saw the deep emotion churning, felt the tension in his shoulders. "Marry me, Evan Masters. Trust me enough to be your partner in life."

The conversation she'd had with him about partnerships came back to her, spiking her emotions. Her grip around him tightened and she smiled. "There's no one I'd rather share my dreams with than you. Yes, I'll marry you."

Ty let out a harsh sigh. "Thank God! I might've taken 'no' for an answer in the past, but this time around I refused to accept anything but a 'yes'."

She tensed and raised her eyebrow, not liking the comparison between Lily and her. "Why?"

Ty pulled her away from the door and gathered her close. "Because I finally found a woman worth fighting for. I've never felt about anyone the way I feel about you, Evan. Plain and simple, you've stolen my heart and captured my soul. I love you."

Evan didn't think Ty could top the emotions he'd just aroused in her, but his declaration turned her heart inside out. She'd never felt so raw or exposed. "I love you, too."

When Ty set her on the ground, she wrapped her arms around his waist and buried her nose next to his neck, hugging him tight.

A tiny, whimpering sound made her tense. The stables were currently unoccupied. At least as far as she knew.

Evan pulled back. "Did you hear that?"

As soon as she spoke, she heard a scratching sound and another whimper.

Ty chuckled and straightened his pants while Evan fixed her skirt. "You had me so caught up, I forgot about the thing I wanted to show you."

He draped an arm around her shoulders, then led her to one of the back stalls.

When Evan's gaze landed on the adorable black Labrador puppy staring at her through the plastic kennel's metal gate, her lips trembled and her heart felt as if it were going to burst from her chest. She loved this man's thoughtfulness so much. "Awwww, he's just adorable!"

Ty walked into the stable ahead of her and unlatched the gate.

The puppy bounded out, jumping right into his arms.

He turned to Evan and put the puppy in her outstretched hands. "*She* has a present for you."

Evan gave him a wary look as the puppy licked her cheek and nibbled at her chin. "When someone says, 'a puppy has a present for you', that usually isn't a *good* thing."

Ty just smiled and turned her chin so she had to look at the dog.

Glancing at the ball of squirming fur, she lifted the pup to rub noses with her and that's when she noticed the dog's red collar had a ring attached to it.

Diamonds lined the silver band, catching the sun's light and stealing Evan's ability to speak.

Ty reached over and removed the puppy's collar. Sliding the ring off, he held it out to her. "I figured a doctor, who takes gloves on and off her hands several times a day, wouldn't have much use for a ring that sat up high, so I thought maybe channel set diamonds would do for an engagement ring. We can get it sized if it's too big."

Tears formed in her eyes once more. Evan's heart filled with love and awe for this wonderful, thoughtful man. She cuddled the puppy under her right arm and held out her left hand for Ty to slide the ring on her finger.

The diamonds glittered even in the low light. Evan held up her hand and grinned at him. "You sure were prepared for a man, who didn't know if I would say 'yes'."

Ty's lips crooked in a sheepish smile as he scratched the puppy behind the ear. "Well, I kind of had a feeling..."

Evan eyed him with suspicion. "What feeling?"

"When I saw you'd placed an ad for an assistant."

Disbelief rolled through her. She had no idea Ty was so impulsive. "You based life-changing decisions on the fact I hired an assistant?"

Ty shook his head, his smile broadening. "No, Doc. I loved you and wanted to help you as best I could."

"How'd you help me?"

Ty replaced the puppy's collar around her neck and rubbed her muzzle. "How do you think I was able to convince my business partner that a long-distance partnership with me making a couple visits to Maryland every month would work?"

Evan shook her head. "I don't know. How did you?"

"Because I told him I'd keep an eye on his baby sister.

After all, I was the one who told her about a great job opportunity that had just opened up in Texas."

Evan's body tensed. "What's your partner's name again?"

"Peter Shannon."

Her eyes grew wide. "Nicole is your partner's sister?"

Ty laughed. "Yep. I remembered Pete had mentioned that Nicole only had one more year to go in vet school, but she was having so much anxiety about her career path once she graduated the following year, that she planned to take a break for a year. So I told her about your job opening and that you were a wonderful lady who had a lot of knowledge to share."

Realization dawned and her gaze narrowed. "Did you put her up to insisting on calling me Doctor Masters?"

Ty raised his hands in innocence. "Nope. Not guilty of that charge." Then he grinned. "But I knew I loved Nicole for a reason."

Cupping her cheek, his expression turned serious. "I would never have given you an animal to shower with love if I didn't think you wouldn't have time to spend with it, Evan."

Evan was speechless. She'd never felt so deeply for another person. Her tears fell onto the puppy's soft coat as she rubbed her cheek against her neck.

"What are you going to name her?" he asked in a quiet voice.

Evan smiled at the puppy chewing on her shirt and kissed the top of her head. Intense emotion welled up as she met Ty's steady gaze. The man had given her so much—love, a future and a companion for life.

"I'll call her Shadow, because she's going to be mine at home and at work. I think my office needs a mascot, don't you?"

Ty wrapped his arms around Evan and the puppy. Holding them close, he kissed Evan on the temple then inhaled next to her neck as if he couldn't get enough of her. "I think that's a great idea, Doc."

I HOPE you loved **TY'S TEMPTATION** and will take the time to leave a review in the on-line store where you bought it. Keep flipping the pages to read an excerpt from book 3 in the **BAD IN BOOTS** series, **COLT'S CHOICE** and following that, an excerpt for book 1, MISTER BLACK, in my *New York Times bestselling* **IN THE SHADOWS** contemporary romance series. And so you don't miss any new P.T. Michelle releases, be sure *to sign up for my newsletter here:* bit.ly/1 1tqAQN

COLT'S CHOICE (BOOK 3) - EXCERPT

BAD IN BOOTS

"Woo-hoo! Ride 'em, cowboy!"

Colt turned in his chair at the feminine calls of encouragement. *Wonder if her body matches that sexy voice?* He bent the blinds to peer out the window. She stood on the bottom board of the fence, leaning over the top rail to cheer his brother on. The position fit her faded jeans to her rear perfectly, displaying all her feminine curves. His gaze traveled to the glossy, jet-black hair swinging against her pink tank top as she watched Mace ride their newest bronco. Must be Mace's bunny-of-the-week. He always had one or two going at a time.

"Damn," he muttered. Shoving away from the desk, he grabbed his hat and headed outside. "Mason!"

His brother landed in the dirt and quickly rolled away from the bucking horse's hooves, while Sam, their wrangler, grabbed hold of the horse's reins and pulled the stallion back to the stables.

"What have I told you about riding the broncs just for kicks?" Colt directed his anger at his brother as he approached the fence. "If Cade wants to risk his neck riding in the rodeos, so be it, but I need at least one brother to keep a head on his shoulders and help me run this place."

Colt didn't give a shit if he came off sounding parental. He'd been responsible for his brothers since he was twenty. He might only be five years older than Cade and seven years older than Mace, but fifteen years and two grown brothers later, he'd found old habits died hard.

Mace picked up his hat, dusted himself off and casually headed toward him. Flashing a quick smile before he settled his hat on his head, he turned to the lady leaning against the fence. "Nothin' I like better than an audience," he said, while his appreciative gaze roamed over her form.

Colt focused his attention on the woman. She couldn't be more than a year or two older than Mace. Lust slammed him hard in the gut as he took in her exquisite features. For once in his life he experienced outright jealousy for something Mace possessed. And it was all wrapped up in a five-foot six-inch, nicely shaped package of sultry green eyes, rosy cheeks, pouty lips and soft, sun-kissed skin. He smiled and the woman returned his smile as she put her hand over the fence toward Mace.

"Nice to meet you," she said as she turned to face his brother, "Mason."

Mace, never one to pass up an opportunity, clasped her hand in his, and instead of shaking it, he kissed her fingers. "Actually, I go by Mace." He grinned. "Pleasure's all mine, Miss...?" He touched the brim of his hat, his eyes carrying a hopeful look.

She gave a throaty laugh at his obvious attempt to find out if she was single. "Miss Elise Hamilton."

Elise Hamilton. Colt stiffened.

"Good to meet you, Elise." Mace raised his eyebrows, then cut an amused gaze his way before he straightened and released her hand. Winking at her, he continued, "I'm sure you and my brother have a *lot* to talk about, so it's off to work for me." He gave Colt a quick salute, then headed for the stables.

"Colt Tanner," he said, putting out his hand. He knew his tone was brusque, but the woman showing up in Texas totally threw him.

"Nice to meet you, Colt." She put her small hand in his larger one and gave a firm handshake.

The last thing he'd expected was for his "partner" to show up here. "You didn't have to come all the way to Texas to sell your half of the ranch to me, Miss Hamilton." He needed to keep the formality. The feel of her hand in his felt somehow right...way too damn right.

She laughed and looked him straight in the eyes, her chin jutting up a little higher. "You're right, it would be ridiculous for me to come all the way to Texas for that, but that's not why I'm here. I'm here because I plan to keep it."

What the hell?

Elise worked hard to keep a straight face, while chuckling inwardly. Her new partner couldn't have been more floored, than if she'd hit him upside the head with a two-by-four. She knew by the gimme-an-effin'-break look on Colt's face that he didn't think she knew her way around a horse, let alone a ranch. She'd been on a ranch before, but one thing was true—she knew absolutely nothing about rodeos. That was why she'd come here. She wanted to learn. Correction, she *needed* to learn. Coming to Boone, Texas was about starting fresh.

She'd noticed the heated look in Colt's steel blue eyes

before he knew who she was. He was attracted to her and, heaven help her, the feeling was definitely mutual. Her gaze traveled up his six-foot two-inch frame. Scuffed leather boots, soft worn blue jeans and a body to die for. Colt Tanner was all viral male.

His white western shirt, a stark contrast to his tanned skin, fit his hard-working muscular body as if it were made just for him. Dark hair peeked out from underneath the black Stetson perched on his head. What would it feel like to run her fingers through that hair? Was it wavy or straight?

With a square jaw boasting late afternoon stubble, his features were more rugged than chiseled, but in her mind those rough edges made him even sexier. The perfect combination of a thin upper lip with a fuller bottom one caused her stomach to drop to her knees.

Unfortunately, right now that mouth had compressed into a thin line, and his jaw muscle jumped with what seemed to be suppressed anger. She wondered if his jaw always did that when he was angry. When her eyes finally settled on his, the deep blue pools, fringed with thick dark lashes, narrowed in obvious irritation.

"Come on, cowboy," Elise began as she moved around him and started toward the stables. Glancing over her shoulder, she cast him a winning smile. "Show me around the ranch."

As she entered the stables and the fresh smells of leather, hay, dirt, horseflesh and open outdoors assailed her senses, Elise knew she'd made the right decision to come to Texas. Inheriting the other half of the Lonestar ranch from her Aunt Marie had given her an opportunity she just couldn't pass up.

So she quit her job—to her father's delight—and then

booked a flight to Texas—to her father's outrage—telling her parents she'd be in Texas for the rest of the summer. Her father was livid. Like that was new. He'd always made it clear he expected her to get tired of her "gallivanting" and then she'd come to work for Hamilton Enterprises, Inc.

She'd shipped some of her things ahead, then driven to Texas, where she'd rented an apartment in town for now. Eventually she planned to rent a house closer to the ranch, but first, she had to convince the other Lonestar owner that she was serious. She had no intention of going back to Virginia. She just hadn't told her parents that yet.

Colt watched Elise walk away, her slim hips swaying. His body immediately reacted to the rhythmic movement as the stirrings of desire slammed into him. He clamped his jaw tighter to keep a rein on his growing attraction to the woman.

Last month he'd been furious when his Uncle James' will was read and he discovered he hadn't inherited the other half of the Lonestar rodeo ranch, as had been agreed upon for the last fifteen years.

Five years ago, his uncle had married, and since then had left the running of the Lonestar completely to Colt, which suited him just fine. But instead of keeping his end of the agreement, upon his death, his uncle willed his half of the Lonestar to his wife, Marie, "to do with as she saw fit". Marie, unfortunately, had decided to give her half of the Lonestar to her niece, Elise Hamilton.

Colt didn't hold anything against Marie. He just wanted the ranch. The sooner the better. He didn't want to the knowledge that his uncle hadn't left him the ranch to leak outside the family. If Riley learned the news, the man would definitely up the ante, doing anything to derail Colt's ability to buy his land back. Their ornery neighbor had always maintained the land was rightfully his.

Throughout the years, Riley had often tried to pit Colt's father and uncle against each other. But blood meant a lot in Texas and even though the two brothers argued from time to time, they'd never wavered in their mutual love or protection of their land.

Once Colt learned the contents of his uncle's will, he'd immediately sought backers to put together a fair offer for Miss Hamilton. Seeking financial help stretched him thin, but would be worth it if he could own the ranch outright. Owning one hundred percent of the property was the only way to guarantee his hold on the Lonestar ranch and surrounding land.

Colt had his attorney draft papers for Ms. Hamilton to sign, selling her half of the ranch to him and he'd overnighted the package to her. He'd never expected her to show up here. She was from Northern Virginia—an elitist society type, from old money.

Her curved backside drew his attention like a magnet, pulling him out of his reverie. The memory of the way her soft hand felt against his a minute ago, a hand that had apparently never known a day of hard work, both aroused and irritated the shit out of him.

Annoyed with himself for being drawn in by her looks, he dropped his gaze to less arousing territory. Dust had just started to form on the heels of her boots. Yep, new as a baby colt and just as shiny. She stopped outside the stables and shook Sam's hand before following him inside the building.

Why was she here?

Maybe she just wanted to have a look-see at her inheritance to make sure it seemed to be run properly. He shrugged. What could showing her around the Lonestar hurt? The sooner he did that, the sooner she could feel the ranch was in capable hands and then be on her way back to Virginia. He'd figure a way to talk her into selling her half of the ranch to him.

By the time Colt entered the stables, Elise was already mounted on Sam's horse. She looked down at him after she'd cast a warm smile at Sam, who stood there holding the horse's reins.

"Sam said I could ride Jack for now and next time he'd saddle up a suitable horse for me next."

Colt turned accusing eyes to his wrangler, who was apparently already bewitched. As Sam looked up at Elise, his smile was so broad his dark mustache bent at a strange angle. Colt gave a loud sigh and moved to saddle his horse. Great, just what he needed, a ranch full of star-struck cowboys who wouldn't get a lick of work done because they were too busy ogling the new part-owner of the Lonestar. Make that the soon-to-be ex-part-owner of the Lonestar, he corrected himself as he swung his leg up on his horse. The sooner he got rid of her, the better all the way around.

As he pulled his horse up next to hers, Colt lifted a spare hat off of a hook on the stable wall and plunked it down on her head none-too-gently. "Here, it'll help keep the heat off," he said in gruff tone, before kicking his heels into Scout's sides to take off ahead of her. He didn't want to think about the fact it also helped hide her beautiful face from the curious cowboys they would meet during their tour.

Colt intentionally galloped ahead. He needed to blow off

steam. Heading in the direction of the open pastures, he figured he'd have to stop and wait for Elise to catch up. He didn't even think to ask her if she knew how to ride. It would serve the "princess" right if she fell off once or twice to show her that ranch life was not easy.

As he started to slow down, Elise came flying past him in a full gallop, the cowboy hat flying off her head. Long black hair streamed and lilting laughter floated behind her as she left him in a cloud of dust kicked up by her horse's hooves.

After stopping to pick up her hat, Colt remounted Scout and dug his heels in, taking off after her. Lowering his head, he spoke to his horse, urging him on. Up ahead, Elise turned her horse to jump a fallen tree. His heart slammed at her reckless move. When she cleared the obstacle with ease, relief and a bit of grudging respect dawned.

Elise slowed her horse and waited for him to catch up. When she turned playful eyes his way, Colt didn't want to like her sultry gaze. He didn't want to wonder if her silky hair felt as soft as it looked. He drew his horse up next to hers, his knee brushing against her thigh as he jammed the hat back on her head. "That has got to be the stupidest thing I've ever seen someone do!"

Her smile faded and she stared back at him in surprise.

Colt rambled on, letting his anger override his libido—or hell, maybe it was because of his libido. "Don't you know better than to try to jump a horse you've never ridden before? How did you know Jack wouldn't have stopped short of that tree and sent you flying?"

Elise's cheeks flamed, then her gaze hardened. "First of all, I'm very familiar with horses. Second, I did think to ask Sam particulars about his horse before I got on him. Third, you have no right to talk to me like that. None whatsoever."

He felt his neck go red at the truth of her last comment, but he and Elise weren't starting off in the most normal of circumstances. He leaned closer to her. "When you're on my ranch, your safety is my responsibility. So yes, Princess, I do have a right to make sure you don't break your lovely little neck."

She gave a knowing smile, then leaned until her nose almost touched his. "I guess it's a good thing the Lonestar is half my property then, isn't it? That way you can absolve yourself of the responsibility."

A challenge had been laid and he'd be damned if he'd pass it up. Colt cupped his hand behind her neck and ignored her cry of surprise as he pulled her mouth to his. Their horses neighed while he explored her lush mouth. His kiss was dominant and hard, just as he meant it to be.

When her resistance melted and she started to respond, his kiss instinctively gentled. He wanted to pull her against him, feel her breasts against his chest, her arms around his neck. He pulled back, angry with himself for wanting to continue, for wanting to know what her sweet body would feel like against his.

"What the hell was that for?" Her eyes flashed, a mixture of anger and desire reflected in their green depths.

Colt sat up straight in his saddle, putting much needed distance between them.

"Just getting that out of the way, darlin'," he said in a rough voice.

He didn't say another word, just turned and trotted off

toward the east side of the property. As far as he was concerned she could follow him or trot her way straight back to Virginia.

Check out Colt's Choice

MISTER BLACK - EXCERPT

IN THE SHADOWS SERIES

Check out a brief excerpt from book one, MISTER BLACK, in my **New York Times** *and* **USA Today** *best selling contemporary romance* **IN THE SHADOWS** *series.*

Straightening, Sebastian takes off his belt and shirt. His breathing saws in and out as he stares down at me for a beat before removing his mask. I'm glad to know I'm not the only one affected. The outline of his broad shoulders and hard, fit body make me want to explore every dip and hollow with my tongue. I'm sad that it's too dark to see more than bits of light play on his face from trees moving in the wind outside, but that means he can't really see mine either.

I reach up and remove my mask. I want to kiss him without it in the way. I don't want anything between us. We'll just hide in the shadows instead.

"Your name," he says, his tone demanding compliance.

I pull my dress over my head, tossing it to him.

My answer.

He crushes the material in a tight fist, then drops it to the floor. Reaching for my ankles, he encircles them, fingers flexing on my skin. Distant lightning flashes, briefly highlighting the top half of his face. The room goes dark again, and all I can picture is the near feral look in his amazing eyes as he tugs me toward him with a powerful jerk, his tone gravelly and full of want. "Then I'll just call you *Mine*."

When he runs his hands up the inside of my thighs, pressing them to the bed with a quiet order, "Keep them here," I comply, eager anticipation curling in my belly. I'm exposed, but he's already seen the ugliest side of me. When I was raw and at my weakest. He just doesn't know it.

Be sure to check out Mister Black

OTHER BOOKS BY P.T. MICHELLE

In the Shadows
(Contemporary Romance, 18+)
Mister Black (Book 1 - Talia & Sebastian)
Scarlett Red (Book 2 - Talia & Sebastian)
Blackest Red (Book 3 - Talia & Sebastian)
Gold Shimmer (Book 4 - Cass & Calder)
Steel Rush (Book 5 - Cass & Calder)
Black Platinum (Book 6 - Talia & Sebastian)
Reddest Black (Book 7 - Talia & Sebastian) - Late Fall 2017

Brightest Kind of Darkness Series
(YA/New Adult Paranormal Romance, 16+)
Ethan (Prequel)
Brightest Kind of Darkness (Book 1)
Lucid (Book 2)
Destiny (Book 3)
Desire (Book 4)
Awaken (Book 5)

Other works by P.T. Michelle writing as Patrice
Michelle

**Bad in Boots series
(Contemporary Romance, 18+)**
Harm's Hunger
Ty's Temptation
Colt's Choice
Josh's Justice

**Kendrian Vampires series
(Paranormal Romance, 18+)**
A Taste for Passion
A Taste for Revenge
A Taste for Control

Stay up-to-date on her latest releases:

Join P.T's Newsletter:
http://bit.ly/11tqAQN

Visit P.T. :

Website: http://www.ptmichelle.com
Twitter: https://twitter.com/PT_Michelle
Facebook: https://www.facebook.com/PTMichelleAuthor
Instagram: http://instagram.com/p.t.michelle
Goodreads:
http://www.goodreads.com/author/show/4862274.P_T_Mic
helle

P.T. Michelle's Facebook Readers' Group:
https://www.facebook.com/groups/PTMichelleReadersGrou
p/

ABOUT THE AUTHOR

P.T. Michelle is the *NEW YORK TIMES, USA TODAY*, and International Bestselling author of the New Adult contemporary romance series IN THE SHADOWS, the YA/New Adult crossover series BRIGHTEST KIND OF DARKNESS, and the romance series: BAD IN BOOTS, KENDRIAN VAMPIRES and SCIONS (listed under Patrice Michelle). She keeps a spiral notepad with her at all times, even on her nightstand. When P.T. isn't writing, she can usually be found reading or taking pictures of landscapes, sunsets and anything beautiful or odd in nature.

To learn when the next P.T. Michelle book will release, join P.T.'s free newsletter http://bit.ly/11tqAQN

Follow P.T. Michelle

www.ptmichelle.com